# Boudin at Trouville

1.

The Beach at Trouville – The Empress Eugénie
1863
Oil on panel, 34.3×57.8cm
Glasgow Museums: The Burrell Collection

Vivien Hamilton

# Boudin at Trouville

John Murray *in association with* Glasgow Muscums

First published in 1992
by John Murray (Publishers) Ltd
50 Albemarle Street, London W1X 4BD
in association with Glasgow Museums

BOUDIN AT TROUVILLE
an exhibition sponsored by the Whyte & Mackay Group

The Burrell Collection, Glasgow Museums, Glasgow
20 November 1992 – 28 February 1993

Courtauld Institute Galleries, University of London, London
15 March – 2 May 1993



A catalogue record for this book is available from the British Library

John Murray ISBN 0-7195-5172 2
Glasgow Museums ISBN 0-902752-49 9

Designed by Peter Campbell
Printed by Butler and Tanner Ltd,
Frome and London

# Contents

*Acknowledgements*

I should like to thank all staff and colleagues of the undernoted museums and libraries for their patient help during the preparation of this book and for their generous assistance in the organization of the exhibition: The Ashmolean Museum, Oxford; The Art Institute of Chicago; The Barber Institute of Fine Arts, University of Birmingham; Berwick-upon-Tweed Borough Museum and Art Gallery; Bibliothèque d'Art et d'Archéologie, Paris; Bibliothèque Nationale, Paris; The Bowes Museum, Barnard Castle;The British Museum, London; Courtauld Institute Galleries, University of London; The Fitzwilliam Museum, Cambridge; Graves Art Gallery, Sheffield; Herbert Art Gallery and Museum, Coventry; Kirkaldy Museum and Art Gallery; McLean Art Gallery and Museum, Greenock; Manchester City Art Gallery; Musée des Beaux-Arts, Le Havre; Musée Eugène Boudin, Honfleur; Musée du Louvre, Paris; Musée d'Orsay, Paris; Musée de Trouville, Trouville; The National Gallery, London; The National Gallery of Art, Washington; The National Gallery of Scotland, Edinburgh; The National Museum of Wales, Cardiff; National Trust for Scotland, Edinburgh; Paisley Museum and Art Gallery; Perth Museum and Art Gallery; and Southampton City Art Gallery.

For assistance in tracing works in private collections, negotiating loans and obtaining photographs I am grateful for the exceptional help I have received from: Anne and Jean-François Apesteguy, Galerie Apesteguy, Deauville; Neil McCrae of Christie's, Glasgow; Tim S. Bathurst and Mrs Susan Ward, of David Caritt Ltd, The Artemis Group, London; Desmond L. Corcoran, Alex. Reid and Lefevre Ltd., London; Richard Green and Victoria Law, Richard Green Fine Art, London; and Simon Matthews of Arthur Tooth & Sons, London.

The mighty tomes that form the *catalogue raisonné* of Boudin's oeuvre were the patient work of Robert Schmit – without them neither this book nor the exhibition would have been possible. In addition, both Manuel and Robert Schmit, Galerie Schmit, Paris, have been of invaluable assistance with loans and photographs, and have offered much advice and kind hospitality.

I was able to spend two valuable months in the USA as a result of having been awarded the Thyne Scholarship for 1991 by the English Speaking Union in Scotland. My special thanks go to George Edwards and Brian Gorman for having made this research trip possible. My thanks also go to the many private lenders who wish to remain anonymous; to John House, Laurent Manoeuvre and Liz Arthur for their excellent contributions to this book; to Moyra Peffer, Patricia Bascom, Rosemary Watt and Nick Pearce for having read the text and made sensible suggestions for improvement; to Ian McWalter of Lexus, Glasgow, for his translations; and to Peter Campbell, Gail Pirkis and John Murray for their patience and professionalism.

As ever, my thanks go to Mum, Anne, Ron and Raymond for their love and understanding.

Finally, I wish to thank my colleagues on the staff of Glasgow Museums for their help, support, encouragement and hard work.

# Boudin at Trouville Exhibition

We at Whyte & Mackay are delighted to sponsor the exhibition 'Boudin at Trouville' at the Burrell Collection in Glasgow and the Courtauld Institute Galleries in London.

Eugène Boudin is widely regarded as the father of Impressionism and his work covers a span of fifty years. He is most famous for his beach scenes at Trouville in Normandy and this exhibition explores, for the first time, Boudin's fascination with life in and around this coastal town.

Boudin's works are seldom seen by the public, as most are held in private collections. Through extensive research, Glasgow Museums has succeeded in bringing together a selection of the best of his paintings on the Trouville theme for this exhibition.

As a Glasgow-based organization, we are pleased to be associated with Glasgow Museums once again. We are particularly pleased that 'Boudin at Trouville' is also showing in one of London's most prestigious galleries, acknowledging the international importance of this major exhibition.

We are confident that visitors will have much pleasure in exploring Boudin's impressions of life in Trouville in the late nineteenth century.

Michael Lunn
*Chairman & Chief Executive*
*Whyte & Mackay Group*

WHYTE & MACKAY GROUP

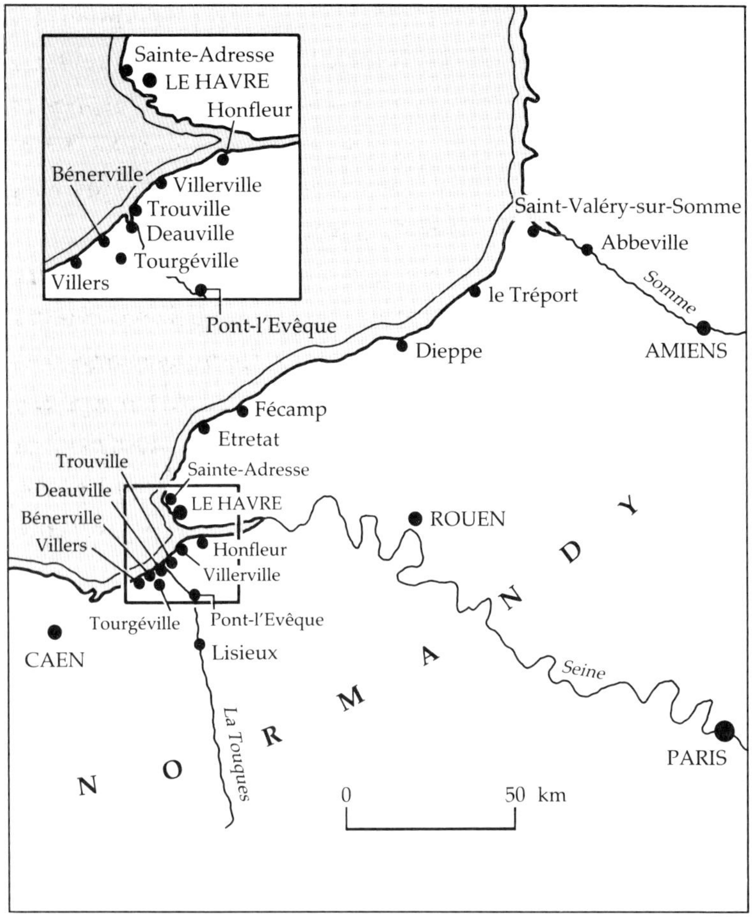

Sainte-Adresse
LE HAVRE
Honfleur
Bénerville
Villerville
Trouville
Deauville
Tourgéville
Villers
Pont-l'Evêque
Saint-Valéry-sur-Somme
Abbeville
Somme
le Tréport
AMIENS
Dieppe
Fécamp
Etretat
Trouville
Sainte-Adresse
Deauville
LE HAVRE
Bénerville
ROUEN
Villers
Honfleur
Villerville
Tourgéville
Pont-l'Evêque
CAEN
Lisieux
Seine
PARIS
La Touques
N O R M A N D Y
0 50 km

# 1. Boudin: An Introduction

2.
Eugène Boudin at Trouville-Deauville
June 1896
Photograph
Musée Eugène Boudin, Honfleur

Throughout his life Eugène Boudin (1824–98) worked ceaselessly and single-mindedly in his struggle to transcribe what he called 'the simple beauties of nature'. His notebooks and letters reveal an artist in pursuit of perfection, eternally frustrated by his feelings of inadequacy before the splendours and wonders of the ever-changing sea and sky. 'I feel this vastness, this delicacy, the brilliant light which transforms everything to my eyes into magical bushes and I can't make my muddle of colours convey this.'[1]

The task he set himself was not a simple one – to capture the restless motion of water and clouds, the transient gleams of light playing on waves, the characteristic movements of the human figure and of ships, and the infinite nuances of colour in the landscape. His achievement, and his originality, lie in the fact that his paintings reveal and record the many moods and effects of an atmosphere which in unifying the scene before him gives his paintings balance, stability and an intimate harmony. As Boudin himself wrote, it is not 'one part of a painting which should grab the attention but the whole; one part is not enough to make a substandard whole acceptable'.[2]

In a career that lasted just over half a century Boudin produced over 4,000 paintings and more than 7,000 drawings, watercolours and pastels. On one occasion, accused of being over-productive, Boudin replied, 'I could work less but then what would I do in between? I would get bored. My only pleasure is painting.'[3] Struggling throughout the 1860s to earn a living from his art, he was delighted when success eventually came. Despite close ties with his dealer Durand-Ruel, he reserved the right to continue to sell works to the private collectors who had supported him earlier and to anyone who wanted a painting simply because they liked it.

If Boudin is classed today as a *petit maître*, it is a position the modest artist himself would not have challenged. When asked to furnish biographical details for a critic in 1887 Boudin wrote that he had 'done various series of seascapes in different genres, beaches which demonstrated if not great art at least a reasonably faithful reproduction of the people of our age'. He finished his brief sketch by saying, 'I have gone on too long about myself, sir – please believe that I do not claim to hold such an elevated position amongst my contemporaries. I am a loner, a daydreamer who has been content to remain in his part of the world and look at the sky. The future will treat me as it does all of us. I am very much afraid it may be oblivion.'[4] Even his biographer, Jean-Aubry, admitted that Boudin's life, which he described as one of 'work, order and patience', was unlike the lives full of 'fantasy, contradictions and passionate violence' associated with the great masters. Boudin's quiet determination and dedication were commented upon in his obituary in *Le Figaro* of 9 August 1898: 'Boudin was a pure painter, a good painter who knew and lived for nothing other than his art . . . His life as a painter was given over entirely to work. He was a man of few words with a great deal of common sense, not full of his own importance, a tireless worker, not really enjoying anything except painting.'

Louis Eugène Boudin was born on 12 July 1824, in a small house on the narrow and winding rue Bourdet, in the port of Honfleur in Normandy. The family moved to Le Havre in 1835 where Boudin was enrolled at L'Ecole des Frères. In 1838 Boudin's father, a sailor, joined La Compagnie des bateaux de Honfleur aboard *Le Français*, one of the first steamers which travelled between Le Havre and Honfleur. His wife worked as a chambermaid for the same company.

Boudin left school in 1836, working first as an assistant in a printer's shop, then for the stationer Alphonse Lemasle. In 1844, he and Jean Acher, who had been Lemasle's foreman, founded their own stationery business at 18 rue de la Communauté, Le Havre. In addition to the usual stock, they also made and sold frames and mounts and, unusually for the time, specialized in selling sketching blocks and paper for pastels, thereby attracting a regular clientele of artists.

It is not known when Boudin first started drawing but it was apparently Lemasle who encouraged his talented assistant by presenting him with a paintbox. In 1845 Boudin showed some of his work to the artist Jean-François Millet, who in vain tried to dissuade the young man from becoming an artist. That decision, however, was partly taken for him, in 1846. He was forced to resign from his partnership with Acher because he needed to withdraw a sizeable sum of money from their business to buy himself out of military service.

Boudin's family was not wealthy and it must have been a burden to have to support him once more. In 1847 he set off for Paris where he studied at the Louvre and made many contacts without actually enrolling in a studio. Exhibiting in 1850 at the *biennale* of La Société des amis des arts du Havre, his work was noticed by the purchasing committee. A petition, supported by references from Troyon and Couture, was sent to the Municipal Council recommending that a study grant be awarded to the self-taught artist. In February 1851 Boudin received a grant of 1,200 francs per year for a period of three years to study painting in Paris.

3.
Eugène Boudin
1890
Photograph
Private Collection

Boudin's letters to his brother Louis and to his friend in Le Havre, Ferdinand Martin, reveal the extent of the privation and hardship that Boudin experienced when his grant finished in 1854. He never wavered from his purpose, however, perpetually aware of his failings but determined to improve his technique. From this time he adopted a pattern that he observed until the end of his life, spending his summers painting outside directly from nature and his winters finishing his paintings in his studio in Paris.

Boudin's choice of a place to work was bound up with his love of the sea. Although throughout his life he continued to paint on his native Normandy coast, almost every year he spent a few months further afield. Initially visiting the Atlantic coast of Brittany in 1855, staying at Quimper, Audierne and Douarnenez, he was to return to the region on more than twenty occasions. At first unhappy with the rugged and unfamiliar countryside, his appreciation of it increased as he grew to understand its people and their customs. His marriage to a Breton girl, Marie-Anne Guedes, in 1863, enhanced his enjoyment of the region. Together they explored the south-west and western coasts at Plougastel-Daoulas, Hanvec, Le Faou, Brest, Kerhor, Landerneau and Hôpital, Camfrout, and later the northern Channel coast of Portrieux, Paimpol, Binic and Saint-Brieuc. Boudin was as fascinated by the weddings and *pardons* (religious festivals in Brittany) as by the markets, the countryside and the coastline.

Boudin's subject-matter would remain essentially the same wherever he worked but, on the whole, the places he visited were chosen precisely because they offered a new aspect of a familiar subject. Eventually he explored other areas of northern France, visiting Dunkerque, Boulogne, Etaples, Berck, Picardy, Le Crotoy, Saint-Valéry-sur-Somme, Abbeville, Le Tréport, Dieppe, Fécamp and Etretat. He first travelled abroad, to Belgium, in 1849. Because of the Franco-Prussian War he again left France, in 1871, drawn to Brussels and Anvers by the promise of sales. He paid further visits to Brussels in 1874 and 1875 and visited Anvers regularly throughout the 1870s and until 1889. Given the nature of his subject-matter it is not surprising that he also travelled to Holland, working in Rotterdam, The Hague, Scheveningen and Dordrecht. Tempted by the beauties of Venice he paid his first visit in 1892, returning for two very productive seasons in 1894 and 1895.

It was ill-health, however, that prompted his visits, near the end of his life, to the south of France. Although he enjoyed the bright sunny weather and the light there he regularly wrote of his preference for the colder and windier Normandy coast. Given the choice Boudin would always elect to be near the sea. In June 1894, when his pupil and friend Louis Braquaval asked where he would visit next, Boudin replied, aware of the irony of the situation, that his doctors had advised him to visit a spa but that 'to see the thing which attracts me most I preferred to head for the sea . . . they want to send me to the Vosges, to Vittel to drink water – me, a man who likes only salt water – imagine my predicament'.[5]

It is interesting that, despite spending each winter in Paris, he never once painted a view of the city. His letters from the capital regularly mention his longing for the sea air and 'a little horizon, a corner of sky joining the sea, clouds, a patch of sea, those little things which are so close down there in the cabin with the red roof. Now I only have that on my pieces of canvas, which is poor consolation.'[6] Nevertheless, he firmly believed that it was vital for an artist to work in Paris, writing to Martin that this 'Paris, this devil of a city, is really the only place where you can develop your skills. There is an example with each step you take and people who encourage you to move forward.'[7] In a letter to his brother some years later he pointed out that 'You don't invent an art all on your own in some corner of the provinces – you need criticism, means of comparison, firm convictions.'[8]

Boudin was successful, unlike many of his Impressionist friends, in having his work exhibited first at the Paris Salon and then, from 1890, at the rival Salon of La Société nationale des beaux- arts. His small paintings presented no challenge to contemporary taste and, given that practical considerations were paramount, took up little space. In addition, he exhibited in the provincial exhibitions in Le Havre, Rouen, Versailles, Lyon, Pau, Strasbourg, Amiens, Bordeaux, Roubaix and Toulouse, remaining loyal to them even when he no longer needed to exhibit in order to sell his work. In the early years, and then again later when there was a crisis in the art market, Boudin resorted to selling his paintings by auction, though this could be an expensive failure. After the struggles of the 1860s, however, he soon discovered collectors eager to purchase his work, and in the dealer Durand-Ruel he found a regular source of income and someone who was not only keen to promote his work in one-man shows in Paris but who was also prepared to take his paintings to Britain and the United States.

Boudin's small works did not attract much critical notice – even though no less a critic than the poet Charles Baudelaire wrote enthusiastically about his pastels in 1859. From time to time, however, his work was admired and received good notices from critics as distinguished as Castagnary, Zola and Duranty. No one was more surprised than Boudin when articles on him were published, commenting that 'I am not used to these fine words from the writing public.'[9] His sense of humour and modesty are evident when, on the occasion of his first one-man show in 1883, he describes himself to Martin: 'There is

4.
Eugène Boudin
Photograph
Private Collection

5.
Eugène Boudin
Photograph
Private Collection

the poor, serious seascape artist and they're calling him a master in some articles, declaring him to be a personality of our times, a lover of the sea and a thousand things which would make me vain if I was capable of such a failing. The surprising thing is that I have caused a revelation. I was lost in obscurity and now I have emerged into the spotlight . . . It's a good exhibition: 150 paintings and as many pastels, drawings, etc. – it all makes a very harmonious whole.'[10]

Though glad to be accepted, Boudin had no interest in receiving official recognition in terms of honours. Awarded a third-class medal at the Salon of 1881, he was finally decorated with the Légion d'honneur in 1892. The year before, the artist Alfred Stevens had wrongly believed Boudin to have been decorated already. Boudin calmly replied to him that 'after struggling to meet material needs for some years I feel it is enough that I make a living from my art. I have never wanted anything else, attaching little importance to my merit and not feeling that I am entitled to ask for more.'[11]

Photographs of Boudin suggest the kindly person he certainly was, with his chestnut brown hair, piercing blue eyes and, as a result of having worked outside so much, a dark complexion. His letters reveal him as a considerate sibling, regularly sending money to his less fortunate brother and sister; a loving husband to Marie-Anne who travelled everywhere with him – they never had any children; and a faithful and loyal friend. Devastated by the death of his wife in 1889, after twenty-six years of marriage, he turned to his work and to nature for consolation. At the end of his life, and despite ill-health, he was still working as hard as ever, writing in 1893 that he was working daily 'only returning home to eat and to sleep'.[12] As late as June 1896 he was still seeking perfection: 'If I regain a little strength I am going to start doing skies again and try once more to struggle against this thing which is so difficult to deal with: light . . . the part of it we get on canvas counts for so little.'[13]

His notebooks are full of his thoughts on art as are his letters to his pupil Braquaval. He continually insists on the need to work directly from nature, to draw and to preserve studies for future reference. Despite the seeming spontaneity of Boudin's paintings he was obsessed with the notion of 'finish'. In a letter to Braquaval he says: 'I have told you many times – an impression is gained in an instant but it then has to be condensed following the rules of art or rather your own feeling and that is the most difficult thing – to finish a painting without spoiling anything.'[14]

Boudin was determined to work until the last days of his life and was frustrated when ill-health prevented him. Dying from cancer of the stomach, he wrote to Braquaval from Beaulieu in the south of France in 1898: 'You think that I don't really feel like working

. . . I took the precaution of putting a few canvases in a case in anticipation of a return to good health, but alas, I think that they will remain uncoloured.'[15] A month later, he wants to return to his native shores: 'In a few days we will be leaving this coast which some consider blessed by God but where I could neither warm my poor old bones or get back my strength; I am going to return to Normandy . . . Shall I find my lost strength on my native soil? I think not because I have become totally exhausted – hardly able to walk 100 steps and no longer having the strength to hold my paintbrush, one of the things which causes me most suffering. If we arrive safely we hope to see you at the beginning of June in Deauville. They are sending me there to breath my native air rather than that of the south. Will I be able to do that? I wouldn't want to die here. I'm too far from all my friends and acquaintances.'[16]

Boudin died in his house at Deauville on 8 August 1898 and was buried alongside his wife in the St Vincent Cemetery in Montmartre in Paris. In January the following year an exhibition of his work, organized by Gustave Cahen, was held at the Ecole des beaux-arts. Although some of the works remaining in his studio were auctioned at the Hôtel Drouot in March 1899, a large number of paintings, drawings, pastels and watercolours were given at Boudin's request and through the generosity of his family to the nation and to the museums in Le Havre and Honfleur.

One of the greatest writers on Boudin, Felix Buhot, in an article published in the *Journal des Arts* on 14 July 1900, eloquently summed up the artist's achievement: 'Boudin's art is the kind of art which wins you over, not by its audacity of expression or the obtrusive violence of its touch but by its beauty, which combines intimacy, delicacy and truth; innovative in a way because it developed towards the open air, towards impression. He was one of the few artists capable of retaining a separateness and a discreetness in his rendering of both the play and reflection of light and the outline of people and objects; his palette of greys and blues, his exquisite shading, his consistent harmony were neither conventional nor formulistic – rather, they were an accurate reflection of nature glimpsed sensitively.'[17]

# 2. Boudin's Modernity

John House

In the twentieth century, Boudin's position in the history of art has generally been established in relative terms: he is presented as a precursor of Impressionism, the painter who, on Monet's own admission, opened his eyes to the beauties of nature and the possibilities of landscape painting; Boudin himself is sometimes marketed as an 'Impressionist'. Yet all these verdicts place him from hindsight, and depend on a view of the history of nineteenth-century painting which defines it in teleological terms, as stages in a progress towards naturalism and open air painting.

Recent studies of French nineteenth-century painting have challenged this traditional view: they have shown that the Impressionists' aims and methods were more complex and varied than had been supposed, and have insisted that an overriding concern with Impressionism and open air painting obscures many central issues in the history of nineteenth-century art. In particular, close attention is now paid to the Paris Salon, the huge exhibition, held annually through most of the century, which was the prime means by which artists made their reputations. The paintings shown at the Salon, and the critical debates around them, generated the terms of reference, the criteria, by which paintings were understood and judged; and it is only by examining the Salon, and contemporary criticisms of it, that we can understand the gradual emergence after 1850 of alternative outlets for art, notably through independently organized exhibitions and commercial art dealers.

In this broader context, Boudin's position is of particular interest. Far from representing the pursuit of a single artistic goal, his art and career, particularly during the 1860s, embodied many of the key dilemmas facing painters in those years. In terms of technique, he pursued a shorthand method of transcribing his perceptions of the most fleeting natural effects, and yet he believed that true art was the product of the creative imagination; in his subject matter, he was torn between a fascination with the world of high fashion, on parade on his beloved Normandy beaches, and a feeling for the indigenous customs of rural communities; and in seeking markets for his work, he exhibited at the Salon but also exploited all other possible means of putting his paintings before potential buyers. This chapter will explore his activities from these three points of view – technique, subject matter and markets – and will suggest that, in the ways in which he responded to these dilemmas, Boudin epitomized, perhaps better than any other artist, the problematic issue of modernity in painting in the 1860s.

### *Technique: Impression and Conception*

Boudin's public reputation was launched by Charles Baudelaire in his review of the Salon of 1859, the first in which Boudin exhibited. Yet Baudelaire's focus was not Boudin's exhibited picture, *The Pardon of Sainte-Anne-le-Palud*, but rather the mass of pastel studies of weather effects which Baudelaire had recently seen in the painter's studio. He hailed these as 'prodigious enchantments of air and water', and yet insisted that Boudin well knew 'that all this will have to be turned into a picture, by means of the poetic impression recalled at will, and he lays no claim to be offering his notes as pictures'.[1]

The distinction that Baudelaire made, between sketch and finished picture, was fundamental to Boudin's art throughout his career. He made myriad drawings and sketches in pencil, charcoal, pastel, watercolour and oils, and yet never considered that these could stand in their own right, as complete, autonomous works of art. On occasion later in his career he did exhibit such studies, but only alongside larger and more highly finished oil paintings.

Yet the relationship between these two aspects of his work was never straightforward. In two much-quoted passages in his notebooks, Boudin wrote: 'Everything that is painted directly and on the spot has always a strength, a power, a vivacity of touch which one cannot recover in the studio', and 'Three strokes of the brush in front of nature are worth more than two days of work at the easel [in the studio].' Yet elsewhere in the notebooks he pointed out that 'One can count as direct paintings things done on the spot or when the impression is fresh', and urged himself to 'elaborate [*pousser*] his studies, whether in front of nature or under the impression [of nature].'[2]

At one level, such comments are a simple recognition of the practical limitations of painting out of doors – that transitory effects of weather and light change so quickly that the painter will inevitably have to finish a work from memory, based on the initial notations made from nature. But even in Boudin's outdoor studies there is a crucial division. Most attention has focused on his notes of light and weather; but throughout his career he also made vast numbers of drawings of particular elements and details in the scenes he was studying – of details of clothing, whole figures and groups, of buildings, boats and quays. In the instructions he gave near the end of his life to a pupil, Louis Braquaval, he constantly reiterated that drawing and the close study of details were the essential starting point for the young artist.[3]

Moreover, his sense of the need to *pousser* his studies shows that he also had a notion of the qualities that a complete picture should have, and that these went beyond a mere notation. Elsewhere he gave some indication of what these qualities were. He noted in 1865: 'One should consider one's picture in advance and ponder it well.' In 1866 he wrote that the painter had to go beyond 'the simple and naïve copy of nature', and that his own work lacked 'strength, boldness and magic'. 'Colour, drawing and form', he felt, 'must come together to express an idea.'[4]

The qualities of the complete work of art, then, depended on a combination of colour, drawing and form; and in each of these fields Boudin had to choose between a range of different conventions. In his colour, he consistently adopted the luminous, all-over light-toned palette, pioneered by Corot, which in the 1850s and 1860s was known as *peinture claire* or *peinture grise*; this means of conveying the effects of outdoor light was, Boudin remembered later, very unfashionable in those years, in contrast to the more theatrical, artificial effects sought by most painters of seascapes. [5] This *peinture claire* was to have a crucial influence on the emergence of Impressionism.

In terms of drawing, Boudin felt the rival claims of broad effects and particular details. Throughout his career, he wanted his finished paintings to retain 'the appearance of the sketch', but he recognized that critics accused him of over-elaboration; his concern with drawing constantly led him to reassert the individual elements in his scenes.[6] His paintings themselves testify to the tension between these two ways of conceiving a landscape.

In the compositional organization of his pictures, too, his work reveals two distinct tendencies. In his studies his ambition was to encounter his subjects directly and without preconception; he wrote in his notebooks: 'Do not be afraid of broad effects in the sky and on the sea, tackle them in all their variety and power without worrying about conventions.' [7] Yet he judged his first major exhibition picture by very conventional criteria; he criticized the composition of his 1859 Salon exhibit, *The Pardon of Sainte-Anne-le-Palud*, because 'it has no centre, its interest is scattered, there is no single figure which sums it all up'.[8]

Boudin's explorations of the problematic relationship between artistic convention and direct experience in painting were very characteristic of French painting around 1860.

Even in the field of historical subject painting, Delacroix offered an example of a painter who was seeking to retain the immediacy of the sketch in finished oil paintings; and in landscape painting Daubigny, in particular, and Corot in his studies from nature were presenting images of the natural world with a freshness and directness which rejected the conventions of colour, touch and composition of French neo-classical landscape. Paintings such as theirs were widely discussed as expressions of the personal sensations and impressions of the artists – a vocabulary which Boudin consistently used in describing his own aims. But at the same time Boudin's concern with details of settings and staffage in his scenes related him to another and older landscape tradition, of topographical depictions of celebrated and picturesque places.

The complexities of Boudin's position in the 1860s emerge most clearly in considering his paintings of explicitly contemporary subjects – of fashionable figures on the Normandy beaches. It is these that we must now examine.

### *Subject Matter: The Bourgeois on the Beach*

It was apparently at the suggestion of the marine painter Eugène Isabey that Boudin began in 1862 to paint fashionable holidaymakers on Trouville beach.[9] Isabey had painted similar subjects of fashionable figures on beaches, but had always clad his figures in seventeenth-century costume, in overt reminiscence of the beach scenes of Dutch seventeenth-century painters such as Adriaen van der Velde; Isabey's scenes with contemporary figures had focused on the peasant life of the Normandy ports.

Boudin's other inspiration in tackling this subject was very probably Baudelaire. At the end of his 1859 discussion of seascapes, in which he had written of his visit to Boudin's studio, Baudelaire made a plea for painters to tackle 'the landscape of great cities' and, probably during the following winter, he drafted an essay on the draughtsman Constantin Guys, which was published in 1863 as 'The Painter of Modern Life'.[10] Baudelaire used Guys' art as a pretext for elaborating ideas about modernity in art that he had outlined in his reviews of the Salons of 1845 and 1846. Although Boudin began to paint fashionable figures before Baudelaire's essay was published, the two men remained in contact, and we must assume that he was familiar with Baudelaire's ideas.

Baudelaire's notion of modernity was based on the image of man in the urban crowd, the *flâneur*, scanning, scrutinizing the faces and figures around him, but always retaining his anonymity: passionately engaged with what he sees, yet impartial.[11] The modernity of Baudelaire's vision was not simply a matter of confronting the contemporary urban world, but involved a particular way of seeing and experiencing that world. In painting, Baudelaire's ideas find their closest echo in a work by another of his associates, Manet's *Music in the Tuileries Gardens* (National Gallery, London) of 1862.

Boudin's paintings of holidaymakers treat the social rituals of the fashionable world in a very similar way, observing the groups and clusters of figures with a close attention to nuances of costume and gesture, but standing at a distance, never engaging with any figure as an individual. Even in *The Beach at Trouville – The Empress Eugénie* (pl. 1), the Empress and her attendants are treated with no more attention than the man and woman on the bench to the left, and they are studiously ignored by the pair of dogs on the right; nor can we be sure which, among the fashionably dressed women, is the Empress herself – perhaps it is the woman in white in the centre of the group, though she is in no way distinguished from the rest.

Most significantly, the beach scenes scrupulously avoid the legible anecdotal interchanges which were the stock-in-trade of contemporary genre painting. We cannot read marital narratives or poignant social or psychological interchanges into them, as we so readily can in the two panoramas of fashionable figures on the beach at Etretat which Eugène Le Poittevin exhibited at the Salon in the mid-1860s. Even the two modern life coastal scenes which Boudin's close friend and associate Louis Alexandre Dubourg exhibited at the Salon in 1869 and 1870 are far more specific and legible than any of Boudin's.

The crucial difference from Baudelaire's 'modern life', of course, is that Boudin's figures are placed on the wide expanses of the beach, not in the enclosed, man-made space of the city. For Baudelaire, modernity was inseparable from the experience of city life, and he vigorously expressed his distaste for the countryside. His friend Schanne remembered his conversation in the train on the way back to Paris from Le Havre in 1859: 'I detest the countryside, especially in fine weather. The constant sunlight overwhelms me . . . Tell me about the ever-changing Parisian skies . . . I may hurt the feelings of you landscapists, but I tell you I can't stand water in a state of freedom; I want it to be imprisoned, in a halter, between the geometric walls of a quay. My favourite walk is on the banks of the Canal de l'Ourcq . . . When I bathe, it's in my bath-tub; I prefer a musical box to a nightingale; and for me the perfect state of garden fruit begins only in the fruit-bowl . . .'[12]

In this context, Boudin's beach scenes present a deep irony – the meeting of two alien worlds, the invasion of the natural by the artificial. Read in this way, they mark the start of one of the key developments of the past century, the rise of mass tourism and the ever-easier penetration of local communities by the moneyed and leisured from the world's great cities. The flood-gates opened across Europe and America by the development of the railways in the nineteenth century (Deauville-Trouville station opened in 1863) have been extended still further, across the whole globe, by the development of mass air travel since the Second World War.

Boudin himself provided a vigorous and extended justification of his beach scenes in a letter in 1868: '[I have been congratulated] for daring to include the things and people of our own time in my pictures, for having found a way of making acceptable men in overcoats and women in waterproofs . . . This attempt isn't new, for the Italians and Flemish painted the people of their own times . . . The peasants have their favourite painters: Millet, Jacque, Breton, and that's fine . . . But don't these bourgeois, who stroll on the jetty towards the sunset, have the right to be fixed on canvas, *to be brought to the light*. Between ourselves, they are often resting from hard toil, these men who emerge from their offices and their studies. If there are some parasites among them, there are also men who have fulfilled their tasks . . . '[13]

Here Boudin wittily took up the moral arguments so often used to justify paintings of the hard-working peasantry, and reapplied them to the urban bourgeois, so as to justify his pictures in terms of the 'toil' of the capitalist entrepreneur. But he himself felt none of Baudelaire's commitment to this boulevard culture. From the mid-1850s he made regular trips to Brittany, and after an extended stay there in 1867 he wrote: 'We ended our expedition with a trip to Plougastel where we saw the most marvellous *pardons* imaginable. Must I admit it? This beach at Trouville that till recently so delighted me, now, on my return, seems merely a ghastly masquerade . . . When one has spent a month in the midst of those races devoted to the harsh labour of the fields, to black bread and water, and one comes back to this band of gilded parasites who look so triumphant, one pities them a little, and also feels a certain shame at painting their idle laziness.'[14]

Here, a very traditional notion of the 'authenticity' of the countryside, with its rooted Christian faith and life based on hard toil on the land, is used to condemn the bourgeois holidaymaker; yet his 1868 letter quoted above (ironically written to the same friend) suggests that he was able to still these anxieties. How should we read the different tone of these two letters? The two together vividly illustrate the conflicting notions of 'nature' at play within the culture, and bring out the inconsistencies of the role attributed to the 'country', as both an exemplar of morality and a passive, inert mass alongside the progressive impetus of the city.

Boudin seems to have felt that these two visions of the 'country' belonged to two distinct spheres and two distinct types of painting, though a local peasant population continued to co-exist with the tourists in the Channel coast resorts. He did not bring the two worlds together in one and the same picture, as Monet so wittily did in *The Beach at Sainte-Adresse* of 1867 (Art Institute of Chicago), where the fishermen and their boats on the beach are punctuated by a bourgeois couple sitting near to the water's edge, with the man gazing out to sea through a telescope.

Despite the confidence in his modern subjects which he expressed in his 1868 letter, Boudin came to paint fewer and fewer fashionable beach scenes, and turned his attention increasingly to the ports and harbours of the northern French coast and to the open sweeps of coastline which still lay beyond the reach of the invading tourist.

Traditional accounts have presented the history of French painting from the 1850s to the 1880s in terms of the growing acceptability of contemporary subject matter. Boudin provides a fascinating example of an artist who, for around five years, painted pictures which can be seen as embodying particularly vividly the issues at stake in 'modernity', but then turned away from this to less immediately topical themes. It would, though, be a mistake to see this as a wholesale abandonment of the contemporary, because the port scenes of his later years are a clear expression of France's economic and commercial vitality.[15]

*Marketing Paintings*

Until very late in the nineteenth century, the Paris Salon remained the prime means by which an artist could attract the attention of critics, potential buyers and the wider public. Boudin fully recognized that Salon success was necessary, and exhibited there regularly from 1864 onwards.[16] However, his main specialities were smaller pictures, not the large one-off exhibition *machines* which stood the best chance of attracting attention on the crowded walls of the Salon's big exhibition halls. Though his Salon exhibits were somewhat larger and more highly finished than most of his paintings, he did not put them at the centre of his production. Instead, he sought out all possible alternative means by which he could find a public for his smaller paintings.

In the 1850s and 1860s the profession of art dealer as we know it today was only beginning to come into being. Only a few dealers, notably Goupil, operated from large gallery spaces; most had small shops. Nor did dealers mount formal exhibitions; instead, they showed works to individual clients, and confined their public displays to a few, frequently changed, pictures in their shop windows; it was the array of pictures in the windows of rue Laffitte, the main dealers' street, that Théophile Gautier characterized in 1858 as 'a sort of permanent Salon'.[17]

Dealers fulfilled an increasingly important role in bringing works of art before potential buyers who themselves had no direct entrée into the art world. At the same time, the dealers' small domestic-scaled spaces offered far more favourable viewing conditions for the smaller works which alone could be accommodated in most private residences. One such space was directed by Louis Martinet in the early 1860s, and Boudin's friend François Bonvin, specialist in genre scenes and still lives, wrote to him in 1861: 'Yet another good mark for your idea of holding a permanent exhibition! That picture I brought you a week ago has just brought me to the notice of the ministry. Placed in a big exhibition, this canvas would not, perhaps, have been noticed. *La peinture intime*, large or small, needs a setting like yours.'[18]

After his move to live in Paris in 1861, Boudin sought out dealers who might be interested in his work. Although he had little immediate success, he gradually began to build up a network of connections which allowed him to sell quite regularly; by the late 1860s he was selling to half a dozen dealers.[19] This situation continued until 1881, when the dealer Paul Durand-Ruel sought to gain exclusive rights to Boudin's works. Durand-Ruel had bought from Boudin in 1872, at the time when he was first buying from the Impressionists-to-be, but it was only with a new injection of capital in 1881 that he was able to buy consistently from Boudin and the now-notorious Impressionists.[20] It was Durand-Ruel, too, who gave Boudin his first one-man exhibition in 1883.

However, Boudin also regularly used another important means for propagating his work – through auction sales. Little research has yet been conducted into the practice of artists sending their own work to auction sales and, on occasion, mounting whole sales of their work. Yet it is clear that, after the Salon, display at the Hôtel Drouot, the Paris auction rooms, was the next most important means of bringing works of art before the public. In 1874 the critic Théodore Duret wrote to Pissarro, seeking to dissuade him from mounting an independent exhibition: ' You have still one step to take, that is to succeed in becoming known to the public and accepted by all the dealers and art lovers. For this purpose there are only the auctions at the Hôtel Drouot and the big exhibitions at the Palais de l'industrie [the salon] . . . The Hoschedé sale [where Pissarro's work had recently fetched good prices] did you more good and advanced you further than all the special exhibitions imaginable. It brought you before a mixed and numerous public.'[21]

Boudin first sought to sell his work at auction at Le Havre in 1857; a sale he and Dubourg put on in Caen in 1862 was a disastrous failure, but a sale in 1868 in Paris was,

Boudin reported, 'quite a good success, not in financial terms, which everyone had anticipated, but a success of novelty and esteem among the artists and even among collectors.' His beach scenes sold particularly well, but fellow artists bought most of the pastels. [22]

This distinction, between two distinct types of work and classes of buyer, is significant. Boudin's stock-in-trade was his more elaborated canvases – in 1868 these were mostly fashionable beach scenes; even these were not large, but very much on a domestic scale, and they found their market through dealers or with the type of collector who relished their social observation and dexterity. Indeed, Boudin's Salon paintings of the 1860s were pictures of this type, though among the largest and most highly finished of them. By contrast, the atmospheric studies which, as we have seen, played an important part in his production, belonged to a class of work which appealed especially to the more limited 'insider' public of the art world itself. It was a longstanding notion that artists themselves were the appropriate buyers of informal studies, since they could appreciate their 'artistic' qualities.[23] In 1861, before Boudin began his beach scenes, one reason a dealer gave for not buying his work was that it was 'too artistic'.[24]

Both these types of painting mark out Boudin's rejection of the large-scale public painting by which most artists sought to make their name at the Salon; and both were explicitly geared towards private-sector buyers. In the 1860s, the Impressionists-to-be were still directing their attention to ambitious one-off canvases for the Salon, but in the 1870s they followed the path that Boudin had taken a decade earlier; like him, they distinguished between their more elaborate pictures, for the dealer market, and their more rapid and improvisatory sketches, and they too sold many of these sketches to close associates and fellow artists. [25]

It is in these three areas, then, that Boudin's career provides so revealing an insight into French painting of the 1860s: in technique, in the rival claims of the rapid notation and the picture with a subject and an 'idea'; in his subjects, in his dilemma between a Baudelairean sense of the modern and a feeling for the 'naturalness' of Breton rural life; and in his marketing, in his cultivation of sketches and smaller-scale paintings for collectors as commodities. His modernity lay, not in any place which might be ascribed to him in a retrospective linear narrative of the development of 'modern art', but rather in his singularly close engagement with many of the central contemporary debates about painting.

# 3. Normandy and its Artists

It is difficult, if not impossible, to analyse with any certainty the rich tapestry of influences, both conscious and subconscious, at work on any young artist. The artist's choice of subject matter and technique can be shaped by a variety of differing circumstances ranging from immediate environment, contact with other artists, visits to temporary exhibitions, museums, the art market, books, music and politics to the artist's own health, family, financial situation and even something as mundane as the availability of transport. This is no less so with Boudin.

If at first Boudin painted landscapes reminiscent of the Barbizon artists, still lifes influenced by Chardin and portraits, he very quickly discovered the subjects that he was to make his own – the air, the sea, the sky and, in particular, the ports, the beaches and the light of his native Normandy. Even when he travelled abroad, to Belgium, Holland and Venice, the subjects, if not the light, remained essentially the same. The two most important centres of influence on Boudin were Paris and the Normandy coast between Le Havre and Trouville. In the former he could visit the Paris Salon, the dealers' galleries and, of course, the Louvre. Despite spending almost every winter of his working life there, he was never once inspired to paint a view of the city itself. What he did was to meet the great variety of artists attracted to the area – from those of the classical and romantic tradition, through the Barbizon painters and Realists to the young pre-Impressionists and Impressionists.

The first step for most aspiring young artists arriving in Paris in the last century was to study at the atelier of a respected artist and attempt to gain access to the Ecole des beaux-arts. Boudin never seems to have considered following this traditional approach for neither during his first visit to Paris in 1847 nor, more surprisingly, when there officially as a student with a grant from Le Havre, in 1851–4, did he join such a studio, preferring to work on his own. Writing to his brother Louis in April 1847, Boudin describes how when lost 'in the middle of this great city the only option is to go to a café or a restaurant . . . I prefer to spend my day copying a Ruysdael. I shall not be bringing back a large number of studies as I have observed more than I have sketched, but I shall have benefited from what I have seen.'[1]

6.
Jan van Goyen
An Estuary with Fishing Boats and Two Frigates
*c.* 1650
Oil on panel, 49.5×69.1cm
The National Gallery, London

If Boudin painted many copies of Old Masters, only a few survive and of those few most were commissioned. He copied works by the Dutch seventeenth-century artists van Goyen, Ruysdael, Potter and Cuyp, and by the French masters Chardin, Watteau and possibly Lancret and Joseph Vernet. In a letter to Louis he describes how 'I did not go to the Louvre until Tuesday . . . but I was overwhelmed by the impression it left on me. It will certainly take a lot of courage to paint something worthwhile after seeing so many masterpieces. I have started several copies. We are there at 8 o'clock every morning and hardly stop until four in the afternoon.'[2]

There was much that the young Boudin could learn from the works of Salomon van Ruysdael (*c.*1600/2–70) and Jan van Goyen (1596–1656), two of the greatest masters of Dutch realist landscape in the period before Jacob van Ruisdael. Van Goyen's *An Estuary with Fishing Boats and Two Frigates* (pl. 6) is typical of their work in its simple composition, low horizon, proportion of sky to water and masterly command of near monochrome tones, and in its subject, with its juxtaposition of fishing boats and masted vessels. Similar elements can be found in the work of Boudin, who shares their mood of calm, their realistic rather than emotional rendering of nature, and their use of oil on small-scale panels. Boudin was also aware of the work of his Dutch contemporaries of whom he heard from Cassinnelli and Jongkind and whose paintings he saw during visits to Holland. Their paintings, however, only reinforced what he had already learnt.

After a visit to the Louvre where he studied Guardi and Vernet, Boudin realized what he needed to pursue in his own work: 'solid backgrounds, water etc. Henceforth to try to paint larger paintings and to take greater care over subordinate figures. To be sure to give more substance to my seascapes. Above all, not to hesitate as regards the forcefulness which has to be achieved throughout.'[3] It was not only the works of the Old Masters that influenced him in Paris for here he could also see works by contemporary artists, both French and English, who themselves had been inspired by his native Normandy.

At the beginning of the nineteenth century the picturesque countryside of Normandy, rich in history and architecture, attracted many travellers from France and beyond. Artists and writers, drawn to the small fishing villages and ports of the Channel coast, attempted to capture in words, in oil or watercolour the everchanging skies, the magical light, the movement of the sea and the lives of those who depended upon it. A great variety of books such as Taylor's *Voyages pittoresques et romantiques dans l'ancienne France* and d'Ostervald's *Excursions sur les côtes et dans les ports de France*, illustrated with lithographs specially commissioned from French and English artists, in turn drew even more visitors to the area. English watercolourists known to have visited Normandy in-

7.
Richard Parkes Bonington
Beached Vessels and a Wagon near Trouville
*c.*1825
Oil on canvas, 37.1×52.2cm
Yale Center for British Art, Paul Mellon Collection

clude Turner, the Cromes, the Fielding brothers, Samuel Prout and David Cox. John Sell Cotman made three trips to Normandy between 1817 and 1820, trips which resulted in the publication of his *Architectural Antiquities of Normandy*, London, 1822.

One of the artists invited to contribute to Taylor's volumes was the English-born artist Richard Parkes Bonington (1802–28). Together Bonington and John Constable (1776–1837) were to exert a major influence on the French landscape tradition. Already in 1821 Charles Nodier had said of Constable's *The Haywain*, 'It is water, air and sky.' [4] After the exhibition of *The Haywain* at the Paris Salon in 1824 the course of French landscape painting changed dramatically.

It is difficult to know what works of these artists the young Boudin would have seen. He would have known of them through older colleagues like Isabey and Huet, and would have been aware of their influence, though at second hand, in the works of the Barbizon artists. That he was aware of their importance is clear from a late letter to his pupil Braquaval. 'At the present time there is only one very unusual exhibition of the English school. Turner, Constable and others. I have benefited a great deal from seeing this . . . it is very instructive and we can learn a lot from it.'[5]

8.

Jean-Auguste Gagnery
The Arrival of the Mail-Coach, Honfleur
1832
Oil on canvas, 67×60cm
Musée Eugène Boudin, Honfleur; on loan from
Musée de la Chartreuse de Douai

Bonington spent much of his short life in France where he was friendly, and even shared a studio, with Eugène Delacroix. He first visited Honfleur, Le Havre and Trouville in 1821. When he returned in 1825 he may have worked with Isabey and in the last year of his life had to cancel a planned trip with Paul Huet to Normandy because of ill-health. Even if the young Boudin never saw any of the many oils, drawings and watercolours that resulted from these journeys he must have heard about them from the two

French artists, both of whom he knew. Bonington's choice of subject and elements of his technique as seen in *Beached Vessels and a Wagon near Trouville*, *c.*1825, prefigure many of Boudin's interests, although the younger artist avoided the anecdotal details of the lives of the fishermen and women that are invariably the focus of Bonington's compositions (pl. 7).

The critical reaction to Bonington's works helped prepare the ground for the works of the young French artists coming after him. Although much loved by collectors, the art critics regularly commented on his lack of finish and on the unsuitability of his subject matter. Reviewing the Salon of 1824 Auguste Jal wrote that Bonington's 'paintings are, from a distance of several feet, the accent of nature, but they are, in truth, only sketches. I prefer M. Isabey's pictures. M. Bonington's figures are drawn with spirit, but they are too slack.' [6] The critic Delecluze went further: '[the] exactness and finesse in rendering the wan effects of the sky and sea on the Channel coast are genuinely worthy of praise, but I avow that a sad sky, or a surging sea, or briny fishermen disputing in the middle of a pile of fish have little attraction for me . . . No, I will never believe that in order to please it will suffice to be true.'[7]

Many French artists working within the classical tradition visited the Normandy coast in this period including A.E. Joinville (1801–49), Louis Garneray (1783–1857) and Auguste-Xavier Leprince (1799–1826). Jean-Auguste Gagnery's *The Arrival of the Mail-Coach, Honfleur*, 1832, exhibited at the Paris Salon in 1832, is typical of the work of these artists in its fine descriptive sense, delicate touch and conventional lighting (pl. 8). The accurate description of the local buildings, fishing boats, stage-coach and costumes make this painting a superb document of the life of the small port in the 1830s. Gagnery avoids any real story or incident and is content to evoke daily life, facing the challenge of realistically portraying a crowd, with its mix of locals, sailors and figures dressed in the height of Paris fashion – something that Boudin was to take up twenty years later. In its composition, with the distinctive sails suggested to the right, this painting is close to many of Boudin's watercolour studies of the fishmarket on the quayside at Trouville.

Artists of the romantic school also visited Normandy in this period, including Eugène Delacroix (1798–1863), Eugène-Gabriel Isabey (1803–86) and Paul Huet (1803–69). Isabey and Huet specialized in painting emotionally charged, romantic seascapes animated with storms or shipwrecks, a typical title of a Huet painting being *Stormy Night on the Beach at Trouville*. Huet, a close friend of Delacroix and Bonington, first visited Normandy in 1818, and continued to do so until just a few years before his death. As was true with so many of these artists, such visits were rich in encounters with other artists and

9.
Eugène Isabey
The Beach at Granville
1863
Oil on canvas, 83×124cm
Musée de Laval, Laval

even writers. In 1828 Huet met Isabey at Honfleur and Mozin at Trouville; in 1829 he introduced the novelist Dumas to Trouville and was there again in 1850 with Troyon. Later still he said he had worked near Boudin and had witnessed Monet's early attempts at working outside from nature.

Baudelaire praised Huet's works as 'véritables poèmes pleins de légéreté, de richesse et de fraicheur'.[8] Huet's fascination with atmosphere and light, executing hundreds of studies in watercolour and pastel after nature for each painting, make him an important precursor of Impressionism. In his letters he describes some of the practical problems of transport that could be faced by an artist: 'I arrived by steamer at one o'clock on Thursday after an excellent crossing. You will probably think I am joking, but the day before the whole of Le Havre had gone to the harbour to see the steamer and the passenger boats leaving. There had been a terrible storm . . . '[9] The very artists who discovered these coasts, however, were soon to regret their role in making them known. Huet's son records that during his father's visit to Trouville in 1854 the 'crowds caused him to flee' and so he went on to Villers instead.[10]

Eugène-Gabriel Isabey, a frequent visitor to Honfleur and Trouville, is credited with

10.

Charles Mozin
The Beach at Trouville,
High Tide on a Windy Day
Oil on panel, 27.5×40.5cm
Musée de Trouville

being the person who first persuaded Boudin to go to Trouville to paint the fashionable bathers on the beach. Isabey's *The Beach at Granville*, 1863, shows that, while tackling a similar subject, in his use of historical costume and in the stormy and dramatic weather conditions, his concerns were very different from those of Boudin (pl. 9).

It is possible that the two artists met in Le Havre as early as 1845. In later years Boudin acknowledged Isabey's help and advice. [11] Earlier, however, he had criticized Isabey's heightened and non-realistic colours, and, in a context where he was specifically talking about his own beach scenes, he asked, 'Isn't it pathetic to see serious people such as Isabey, Meissonier and so many others searching out gaudy carnival clothes and because it is supposed to be picturesque using them on models, who as often as not do not know how to carry off borrowed finery?'[12] In the same letter he criticizes Eugène Le Poittevin (1806–70), an artist who combined the romantic taste of Isabey with the descriptive and anecdotal detail of his master Leprince. Boudin wrote despairingly of Le Poittevin as having 'made his fortune with an old plumed hat and a pair of musketeer's boots which he has painted and repainted in every context imaginable. I should be very grateful if one of these Gentlemen would explain to me the interest these objects will

11.

Charles Mozin
The *Invincible* reaching the Port of Trouville
1855
Oil on canvas, 175×270cm
Musée de Trouville

have for future generations and whether the picturesque nature of these canvases will have a powerful effect on our great-nephews.'[13]

Another student of Leprince and one of the first artists to work consistently in Trouville was Charles Mozin (1802–62). Although some of his more romantic and dramatic seascapes draw on contemporary history, as in *The Invincible Reaching the Port of Trouville*, 1855 (pl. 11), many of his paintings – precisely drawn and warm in tonality – are views of the town, the fishing boats or the entrance to the harbour, or are landscapes of cows beside the river Touques. These paintings were exhibited at the Paris Salon from 1827.

During his own lifetime Mozin, rather than the writer Alexandre Dumas, was proclaimed as the true 'discoverer' of the charming little fishing village of Trouville. Albert Blanquet, writing in the *Revue des Beaux-Arts* in 1858, describes how each summer the artists left Paris in search of light, sun, rich landscapes and shadowy forests. Of Mozin Blanquet wrote, 'he was young then, it was 1825, and he was seeking views and solitude; leaving the mud and silt of Honfleur, he arrived, almost without realizing it, among the modest cottages of a little village on the sea. He was intoxicated, charmed, seduced. There he pitched his tent or rather the weird umbrella which looked so strange in the countryside and which provoked such naïve wonder in the countryfolk. For the artist there was a wealth of subject matter to be exploited. None of these places had been observed in this way before, as the countryfolk and fishermen had better things to do than contemplate the land they worked. The result – Mozin put down on canvas all the faces of Trouville with such a love of the peace and tranquillity he enjoyed that merely looking at his landscapes, always bounded by the vast and beautiful sea, is enough to make one yearn to be there.

'Unfortunately for him, he had the misguided idea of sending these paintings to the Salon and to announce them proudly in the catalogue as: *The Beach at Trouville* . . . he showed off this little haven like a doting father – and all was lost.'[14]

In 1839 Mozin built a house in Trouville in the style of an old manor house. He arrived each year in June and stayed until as near the end of the year as possible. The house was situated like an observation post, between the river Touques and the sea, on the Pointe de la Cahotte near the boatyard, allowing the artist to work directly from nature through his studio window. From a letter written by his wife Pauline, we know that he also drew outside: 'Charles is also working. He has made the most of his month of solitude and is at his easel from dawn till dusk. If he goes out, it is to sketch some interesting scene or other, as there is plenty of incident in our little port. Charles is the most dauntless of us, he never feels the cold and makes fun of us when we complain about the temperature. He likes the open air life and it suits him well.' [15]

Mozin was very much involved in the life of the developing town and served as a municipal councillor. He was, however, worried about the changes which he had helped bring about: 'it was in 1825 that I discovered this promised land. It is very different in appearance today, and if the tourist now finds some of the comfort to which I have contributed in spite of myself, he has lost the picturesque, of such charm to the artist who now flees its civilized beach. I thought I could enjoy it like a miser, imagining I could shut myself away from the world in this thatched nest.' [16] Such feelings were shared by other early visitors including the novelist Flaubert, whose short story 'A Simple Heart' is set in the area. But if Mozin worried about the increasing popularity of the town, his own lithographs had surely played a major role in spreading news of its beauties. Invaluable documents recording the changes wrought on a small fishing village rapidly developing to meet the needs of changing attitudes to leisure, they depict the new villas, the hotels, the fishmarket, the port and the beach with its bathing machines.

The very titles of the plates in Mozin's album *Trouville et ses environs* (1 vol. 1844/5 and 2 vols. 1855) read like a summary of the subjects that Boudin was to make his own : *The Fishmarket*, *The Entrance to the Jetties*, *The Bathing Beach*, *The Jetties, from the Sea* and *The*

12.
Camille Corot
Beached Fishing Boat, Trouville
*c.*1830
Oil on panel
Musée d'Orsay, Paris

*Roches Noires from the Beach*. Although Mozin's beach scenes are stylistically close to those of Isabey, his interest in light, in working directly from nature and in capturing the different tides and the times of the day show him moving away from romanticism towards realism. As one critic pointed out Mozin, 'who died two years ago in Trouville, was one of the French painters who best understood the overcast skies and the deep mysterious waters of the Channel'.[17]

*The Beach at Trouville, High Tide on a Windy Day* provides an interesting comparison with Boudin's earliest Trouville beach scenes which are similar in scale and are also oil on panel (pl. 10). As in Boudin's *The Beach at Trouville* and *The Beach at Trouville – The*

13.
Ferme Saint-Siméon, Honfleur
*c.*1854–60
Pastel, 30×46cm
Private Collection. Courtesy of Galerie Schmit, Paris

14.
Ferme Saint-Siméon, Honfleur
1860
Pastel, 20×30cm
Private Collection. Courtesy of
Galerie Schmit, Paris

*Empress Eugénie*, Mozin's painting shows the Casino with its busy terrace and Dr Oliffe's house with its distinctive tower, while the Hôtel de la Mer is just out of sight to the right (pls. 26 and 1). Mozin, unlike Boudin, composed the painting in the studio, choosing a dramatic view of the beach from the sea, a view rarely shown by Boudin. Fascinated by the stormy sea, Mozin shows the tiny human figures pitted against a powerful nature, an anecdotal treatment of the subject of no interest to Boudin. Although it is not known what Boudin thought of Mozin, or whether they even met – Mozin died in the year that Boudin is first thought to have worked in Trouville – there can be no doubt that the older artist, in his paintings and prints, explored the range of subjects that Trouville would provide for Boudin.

Corot (1796–1875), Millet (1814–75), Troyon (1810–65) and the Barbizon artists Diaz (1807/8–76), Dupré (1811–89) and Rousseau (1812–67) were similarly drawn to the Normandy coast. Boudin, who considered Corot and Millet as 'the two greatest individuals of our time', met many of these artists, initially in the framer's shop in Le Havre, then at the Ferme Saint-Siméon in Honfleur and in their studios in Paris. [18] From them he learned about light and how to render it with freer brushstrokes. More importantly they encouraged him to work outside, directly from nature.

In 1829 Corot wrote that '. . . I am setting aside the month of August to visit a little place called Trouville which has an abundance of charming motifs.' [19] One of the many paintings that resulted from this visit was *Beached Fishing Boat, Trouville*, *c.*1830 (pl. 12), which in its subject and treatment anticipates many works by Boudin. Corot is known to have admired the younger artist, calling him *le roi des ciels* and keeping, throughout his life, a pastel study of a sky that Boudin had dedicated to him.

Troyon, who specialized in market scenes and landscapes with cows, inspired Boudin's many canvases of similar subjects. Boudin's *Trouville Road* is close in composition and handling to many works by Troyon (pl. 85). Troyon visited Normandy regularly from the mid-1840s, captivated by the changing skies and the magnificent light. Much in vogue in the early 1860s, and struggling to meet the demand for his work, he paid Boudin to work for him. This was a valuable source of income for Boudin and also provided him with the chance to work on large-scale canvases and so broaden his technique. Troyon also offered to help sell some of his work, though it is clear that Troyon's notion of what constituted 'finish' was different from that of Boudin. In May 1859 Monet wrote to Boudin from Paris, saying 'Troyon talked to me a lot about you. He is amazed not to see you in the capital. He has asked me to tell you to send him ten or so of your most finished paintings, grey seascapes, still lifes, landscapes. He says he will find buyers for them if they are more finished than the ones he has had from you previously.'[20]

One of the most popular meeting places for artists visiting Honfleur in the 1850s and '60s was the Ferme Saint-Siméon run by Mère Toutain. Just as the older artists enjoyed the magnificent views from the Côte de Grace over the sea, the cider and the seafood consumed at trestle tables in the orchard, so did the younger generation of artists – Courbet, Jongkind, Monet and Bazille. Near the end of his life Boudin recalled his stays at Saint-Siméon where he was, he said, the first lodger, paying 40 francs a month for board and lodging.[21]

One of Boudin's closest friends was the artist Théodule Ribot (1823–91). The two artists first met in Le Havre in 1851. Ribot, known for his Spanish-influenced genre scenes and portraits, also painted seascapes near Honfleur and Trouville where he frequently joined Boudin. In April 1865, Boudin, in a letter to his brother Louis, describes how Ribot had been a magnificent help, encouraging him to persevere in his own path despite the advice of others. Many years later Boudin wrote to Ribot that he could not 'resist the temptation of sending you my sincere congratulations on your very good exhibition which I went to last night . . . It is a consolation for us to see that in spite of our advancing years we are still valiantly holding our own against the unruly and daring

15.
Gustave Courbet
Woman with a Parasol – Portrait of
Mlle Aube de la Holde
1865
Oil on canvas, 92.1×73.7cm
Glasgow Museums: The Burrell
Collection

young people who do not want to do the same as their predecessors and who perhaps are getting a little carried away in their fracturing of colour and light.'[22]

Another friend who shared the pleasures of the Normandy coast and the hospitality of the Ferme Saint-Siméon was Gustave Courbet (1819–77). Writing in 1878, Boudin said that there are 'certain people to whom you feel inexplicably drawn, people who captivate you to a greater or lesser extent. Courbet was one of those.' Imprisoned in 1871 for his role in the destruction of the Vendôme Column, Courbet was deserted by many of his artist friends but not by Boudin who wrote to assure him that he was in his thoughts. Their friendship dated back to a meeting in Le Havre in 1859, described by Courbet's friend Schanne. Walking in the rue de Paris, Courbet and Schanne saw 'in the window of a stationer's small seascapes conscientiously done on panel' and asked for the address of the artist. Boudin, delighted by this unexpected visit, immediately offered to be their guide and the three set off for Honfleur.[24] It was during this visit that they met the poet Baudelaire to whom Boudin showed his pastels.

Boudin recorded something of what was discussed in his notebook, saying that if he was to believe them 'I would without doubt consider myself as one of the talents of our age. He [Courbet] felt that the tone of my painting is too weak, which may be true, strictly speaking; but he assured me that few people paint as well as I do.'[25] A few days later he records how they had had a rowdy and drunken evening at Dreuil's and the following morning 'we were heavy headed but that didn't prevent us admiring beautiful things, to such an extent that I have resolved to stay there [Honfleur?] this summer if I can. Courbet has already freed me of a little of my timidity; I will try large paintings, large subjects with more attention to tone. In short, we are plunging wholeheartedly into art. Courage!' He goes on to say that he has been watching Courbet working but that the latter's large brushstrokes would not suit his own art: 'that seems decidedly crude to me, with little attention to detail'.[26] Boudin, on Courbet's advice, tried to work on a larger scale and with broader handling. The influence, which worked both ways, was commented upon by their contemporaries.

Zola, reviewing the Salon of 1868, wrote that at 'that time when he [Courbet] was painting what he called *paysages de mer*, he met a painter who had a feeling for watery horizons, water and the vibrant splashes made by a woman's dress against a grey sky. I am talking about Boudin who has two excellent paintings at the Salon. *Setting off for the Pardon* is a little out of character for the painter. I prefer the *Jetty at Le Havre*. There I see the artist's exquisite originality, his large silver-grey skies, his little figures so fine and witty of touch. There is a rare accuracy of observation in the details and attitudes of these figures grouped on the edge of the vast expanse. It is charming and conveys a charming and true impression. Together with Manet, Jongkind and Claude Monet, Boudin is definitely one of today's best seascape artists.'[27] Cousin Pons writing in *Le Figaro* in May 1891 about the Arosa sale describes a Courbet as 'a superb landscape. No evidence of the impasto for which the painter is criticized. The painting is precise, clear and sure in its planes. When you look at this important though small painting you sense the influence which the old master Boudin had for a short time on the painter from Ornans.'[28]

That moment had probably happened during the months Courbet spent in Trouville in the summer and autumn of 1865 and 1866. It was doubtless at this time too that 'Courbet, leaving his canvas, leant slightly over towards Boudin who was sketching the same subject – sea and sky. "It's incredible", cried Courbet shrugging his powerful shoulders. "My dear fellow you must be a seraph; you are the only person to really know the sky." '[29] Courbet's letters to his family and friends describe his luxurious lifestyle in Trouville and the popularity he enjoyed. They marvellously evoke the social life of the town, but one that Boudin possibly did not participate in. Although there are one or two brief mentions of his wife bathing for the sake of her health during visits to Brittany we never learn whether Boudin himself bathed nor do we know if he ever even visited the Casino. Unlike Courbet, Boudin had abandoned portraiture, and despite his splendid small beach scenes, so popular today, seems to have had no entrée to the elegant and rich society that he painted.

In a letter to his father Courbet describes how he has 'made the acquaintance of all these people who may be useful to me. I have had over two thousand women visiting my studio; they all want to be painted . . . I have done thirty-five pictures, which has astonished everyone. I have bathed in the sea eighty times; only six days ago we went bathing with the painter Whistler, who is with me here.' [30]

Writing in the *Gazette des Beaux-Arts* in September 1878, Paul Mantz described how, during the 'finest days of the summer of 1865 Courbet spent some time in Trouville. He had solitary conversations with the ocean; it was then that he started the series of marine studies which he was to continue the following year and which did him such credit. He did not just see the sea, he also looked at the attire of Parisians on vacation with the interest an artist must show in anything eccentric. Fascinated by the elegant fashions, he did not miss the opportunity to paint some portraits.'[31]

One of the portraits executed during Courbet's first stay is *Woman with a Parasol – Portrait of Mlle Aube de la Holde*, 1865, which like his portrait of the Comtesse Karoly de

Hongrie combines portraiture with a magnificent sunset seascape (pl. 15). Courbet refers to it in a letter of 16 September to Urbain Cuenot at Ornans: 'here in Trouville I am in a delightful position. The Casino has offered me a superb apartment looking out over the sea and there I paint the portraits of the most beautiful women in Trouville. I have already painted the portrait of the Countess Karoly of Hungary; this portrait was an unprecedented success. Over 400 ladies came to see it and ten or so very beautiful ladies want their portraits painted. At the moment I am doing one of Miss Haube de la Holde, a young Parisian girl who, in a different way, is just as beautiful as Miss Karoly.

'I am paid 1,500 francs each for these portraits . . . I still have to do another seascape for the Comte de Choiseul . . . I shall not be able to leave Trouville until the end of the season.

'I have earned myself a reputation as an unrivalled portrait painter. The portraits which I am unable to paint here will be done in Paris this winter. So I find myself with an enormous clientele.

'. . . I don't really have the time to write. There are so many people around me that I can't hear what any of them are saying. You made a great mistake not coming to Trouville. The weather is splendid and the bathing too. I sometimes bathe twice a day; it is as warm as in summer.' [32]

As Courbet expected, such contacts were indeed useful to him. In January 1866, the Comte de Choiseul and his sister, the Marquise de Montalembert, visited Courbet's Paris studio to buy some of his seascapes. That same year he was invited to stay as their guest at the comte's luxurious villa in Deauville.

> My dear Boudin,
>
> At the request of M. de Choiseul I invite you and your wife to dine with us tomorrow, Wednesday, at six in the evening. I have already invited M. Monet and his wife who promised me last night at the Casino that they would come. I trust that you will do us the honour of accepting.
>
> Best wishes,
> G. Courbet
> Châlet Choiseul
>
> Pick up Monet on your way and come together, the four of you. I shall expect you without fail.[33]

Courbet's generosity meant that Boudin too was now given an entrée into this fashionable and wealthy circle and it is surely no coincidence that the following year the Comte de Choiseul bought a *View of Deauville* by Boudin.

Today Boudin and the Dutch artist Johann Barthold Jongkind (1819-91) are acknowledged as the most important precursors of Impressionism. Their key role in the development of French landscape painting was recognized even in their own time: 'Boudin is one of those to whom contemporary art owes a debt. He shares with Jongkind the honour of having speeded up the evolution of the landscape in the direction indicated by our celebrated Corot.'[34] Gustave Geffroy, reviewing Boudin's exhibition at Durand-Ruel's gallery in February 1883, wrote that Boudin 'is, together with Corot and Jongkind, one of the immediate precursors of Impressionism. He shows us that impenetrable black does not exist and that air is transparent.'[35]

Contemporary critics and artists alike proclaimed Jongkind's importance. Edmond de Goncourt claimed that all 'the landscapes which are worth anything at the present time are based on this painter, borrow his skies, his atmospheres, his locations. It is obvious yet no one says it.' [36] Emile Zola wrote that an artist 'of such awareness and such originality is a master, not in a flashy and ostentatious way but in an intimate way, penetrating with a rare flexibility the multi-faceted world of objects.'[37] Monet too was aware of Jongkind's influence. He wrote that one 'has always something to gain from studying Jongkind's landscapes because he paints what he sees and what he feels with sincerity'.[38]

Like Monet, Boudin admired Jongkind, '[who was] my master from this moment on and . . . who trained my eye once and for all', and was frustrated that his friend was never awarded the Légion d'honneur. [39] Both artists shared an interest in the analysis and notation of light, and a love of the coast with its ports, boats and ceaselessly changing water. While Jongkind's works are more precise, more varied and much warmer in tone, both strove to achieve a feeling of space and capture an all-enveloping atmosphere. Of all his contemporaries it is possible that the only one to have influenced Jongkind was Boudin.

It was through the influence of Isabey that Jongkind first visited the Normandy coast in 1847, eventually meeting Boudin there in 1862. In 1863 Jongkind, in Paris, wrote to Boudin that he had 'often thought of my trip last year and of all the tokens of friendship when I made your acquaintance in Honfleur and in Trouville'.[40] Boudin, Jongkind and Monet were to be particularly close in the period 1862–5 when Jongkind spent his summers at Honfleur. Their friendship is documented in the surviving letters from Jongkind to Boudin from 1862 to 1883. Unfortunately Boudin's letters have not survived, a fact made more distressing by a phrase in one of Jongkind's replies, where he writes that he considers Boudin's letter 'an item of great poetry and reverie . . .'[41]

Prior to their first meeting with Jongkind it is clear that both Monet and Boudin knew of Jongkind's work, the former writing to urge Boudin to come to Paris in 1860 saying, though mistakenly, that 'you could only benefit from it. You know that the only

16.
Johann Barthold Jongkind
Etretat
1865
Oil on canvas, 28×38cm
Private Collection; photo courtesy of Hazlitt Gallery, London

good seascape artist we have, Jongkind, is dead to art: he is completely mad. Artists are donating money to meet his needs. There is a nice position waiting for you.'[42]

Jongkind's letters from Honfleur are interesting in reminding us that, although the artists were working only a few miles from one another along the coast, regular meetings were difficult, invariably the problems being the weather, transport and shortage of funds. From his letters we know not only that Jongkind loved the coast and the busy port, but also that he, like Boudin, felt he needed to know a place well before he could paint it. He regularly states that to make anything solid of his work in Honfleur he will need to return the following year. He delighted in the local cider and enjoyed bathing, though, typical of the time, he implies that the bathing was for the good of his health rather than for pleasure: 'bathing in the sea has done me good but I am still not completely well. It is the result of treatment for my nerves.'[43]

An artist who exerted a great influence on Boudin, particularly in his landscapes, was Charles Daubigny (1817–78). In January 1869 Boudin wrote that he had just been to visit Daubigny and that seeing Daubigny's works made him feel second best for, in his 'studies [there is] a boldness, an abandon which I would like to put in mine'.[44] Frequently accused of sending 'mere sketches' to the Salon, Daubigny was an important influence on the younger generation of artists with his open brushstrokes, and his insistence on working consistently in the open air from nature. Daubigny first visited Normandy in 1854 and from then until his death he and Boudin met regularly at Villerville, Trouville and Honfleur. Together the boldness of Daubigny and the audacity of Jongkind influenced Boudin towards a more open and free handling of paint.

Claude Monet (1840–1926) is revered as the master of French Impressionism. By comparison, Boudin's reputation is slight. And yet, as the elderly Monet proclaimed in a letter to Gustave Geffroy, he considered Boudin 'as my Master'. Monet explains how, when they met at Gravier's shop in Le Havre in 1858, Boudin advised him to stop wasting his time doing caricatures and encouraged him to paint with him out of doors directly from nature. Monet describes how one day, 'Boudin said to me, "You are gifted. Leave this work which bores you. Your sketches are excellent, you musn't stop there. Do as I did – learn to draw well and admire the sea, the light, the blue sky." I followed his advice and together we went on long walks during which I continually painted from nature. That is how I came to understand it and learnt to love it passionately and how I became interested in the clear painting Boudin produced . . . I have said it once and I shall say it again – I owe everything to Boudin and am grateful to him for my success.'[45]

In a letter to Boudin's biographer, Jean-Aubry, Monet further explained how Boudin 'set up his easel and began to paint. I looked on with some apprehension, then more attentively and suddenly it was as if a veil was torn away; I had understood, had grasped what painting could be; by the sole example of this painter absorbed in his art and independence of effort, my own destiny was made clear.'[46] Boudin himself was aware of the role he had played and also that the pupil had long since outstripped the master. Writing to Braquaval in May 1895 Boudin advises him to visit the exhibition of Monet's Rouen Cathedral paintings at Durand-Ruel's, saying that he himself 'may have slightly influenced the group which is moving painting towards the study of great light and sincerity in reproducing the sky's effects'.[47]

That Monet admired Boudin there can be no doubt. As with so many of the artists who knew and worked with Boudin, Monet felt great affection for him, admiring in his art the subtle colours, the mastery of harmony and half-tones, the lightness of the air and the harmony between the atmosphere and the subject treated. Their friendship can be traced in their surviving letters, beginning in the late 1850s and early 1860s when Monet, in Paris, urged Boudin to leave that *sale ville du Havre* and come to the capital to

17.
Claude-Oscar Monet
The Beach at Trouville
1870
Oil on canvas, 37.5×45.7cm
The National Gallery, London

give him advice and visit the important exhibitions. Monet, who saw a definite role for Boudin, never hesitated to point this out. Having visited the Salon of 1859 he described how 'Isabey has produced a horrible concoction. The detail is pretty. There are pretty little figures. There is a complete lack of seascape artists and it is a path which could take you far.'[48] Later, throughout the 1860s and until 1870, they met in Paris in the winter and on the Normandy coast in the summer. Boudin watched the young Monet's career with interest and his letters to Ferdinand Martin provide a commentary on Monet's struggle and eventual success.

Boudin was aware that Monet was breaking new ground and understood, admired and respected him for that. In a letter to Martin of May 1868 he writes that at the Salon 'I met Monet who is an example to us all with the steadfastness of his principles. One of his paintings was accepted to the great horror of certain people; they are wrong because this painting always makes a laudable attempt to find the true tone, an attempt which is beginning to be admired by everyone.'[49] As early as 1872 Boudin, admiring the studies Monet had just brought back from Holland, believed that 'he is destined to become one of the leading figures in our school.'[50] In June 1886 he tells Martin that the day before he had visited an exhibition at Petit's gallery 'where Monet was attracting a lot of attention. That fellow has become so daring with his tones that you can't look at anything after something of his. His paintings overshadow everything else and make it look dated. Never have paintings been more vibrant or intense: if the price wasn't so terrifying for the middle classes they would snatch them up – but the exterior is so hard that few people dare to look underneath.'[51]

The two artists continued to correspond until the end, their letters usually prompted by news of engagements, weddings or deaths. Monet regularly ended his letters with assurances that 'I haven't forgotten that you were the first to teach me to see and to understand.'[52] It has often been suggested that Monet's *The Beach at Trouville*, 1870, shows Monet's wife Camille in white in the left foreground and that the figure in black is Boudin's wife (pl. 17). A late letter is of interest for what it reveals about the period when they worked together in Trouville, in 1870 certainly, but also possibly in the 1860s. Writing to Monet from Deauville on 14 July 1897, Boudin congratulates him on the marriage of his son Jean Monet to Blanche Hoschedé, saying that he had 'kept . . . a drawing which shows you on the beach. There are three women in white in it, still young. Two of them have died, my poor Marie-Anne and your wife. One of the three is still hale and hearty. Little Jean is playing in the sand and his father is sitting on the ground with a sketch in his hand . . . and isn't working. It is a souvenir of that period which I have always treasured.'[53]

Although they worked together, Monet's *The Beach at Trouville* already reveals that, however close the subject matter, their techniques were very different. Where Boudin places himself at some distance from the bathers on the beach, preferring to paint crowds of anonymous strangers, Monet has set up his easel in the very midst of one of these groups, preferring to paint his own family and friends. Unlike Monet, Boudin was not interested in translating figures, objects or light into definite colour. While Monet experiments with broad flat tones of fresh colour, Boudin's palette remains grey, sparkle and vibration being achieved by broken tones and contrasts but not by the division of colour used by the Impressionists. Similarly, while Monet's *Jetty at Trouville, Low Tide*, 1870 (Szépmüvészeti Museum, Budapest), is remarkably similar in its subject to many of Boudin's paintings, the treatment of the painted surface is once more very different.

Despite Boudin's close contacts with Monet and with the dealer Durand-Ruel, and

18.

Louis Alexandre Dubourg
Sea-bathing at Honfleur
1869
Oil on canvas, 50×86cm
Musée Eugène Boudin, Honfleur

19.

Charles Pécrus
The Hôtel de la Mer, Trouville
1875
Oil on panel, 27.2×45.6cm
Musée de Trouville

although he participated in the first Impressionist exhibition in 1874, he does not seem to have been associated with other Impressionists like Sisley, Renoir or Pissarro, nor with Manet or Degas. Manet's *On the Beach*, 1873 (Musée d'Orsay, Paris), and Degas' *Beach Scene*, *c.*1877 (National Gallery, London), show both artists prepared to experiment, if not entirely successfully, with an unfamiliar subject. Like Monet, however, their painterly concerns and their free, broad, almost disjointed treatment of form demonstrate concerns very different from those of Boudin. Although Degas knew Boudin's pupil Braquaval well from the 1890s, and Degas himself purchased works from the sale in March 1899 of Boudin's studio, there is no evidence that the two artists met in Normandy.

There were, however, many artists either born in Normandy or who settled there with whom Boudin was close. Two of the most important were Charles Pécrus (1826–1907) and Louis Alexandre Dubourg (1821–91). Like Boudin, both artists painted the beaches of Honfleur and Trouville with their summer visitors.

Dubourg was born in Honfleur in 1821. After studying in Paris, he returned to his native town and specialized in painting scenes of the daily life of its fishermen, port, beach and the surrounding landscape. A frequent patron of the Ferme Saint-Siméon, in his letters he kept Boudin, then in Trouville, informed of the comings and goings of visiting artists like Monet. It was Dubourg who, in 1868, persuaded the town council to found a small museum to give visitors *le goût des Beaux-Arts* and became its first curator. Dubourg's *Sea-bathing at Honfleur*, 1869, in its detail, theatricality and interest in anecdote, lacks the spontaneity and freshness of his watercolours and oil sketches (pl. 18). The broken brushstrokes, light tones and sensitivity to atmosphere, however, show his awareness of the challenges of Impressionism.

His other close friend, Pécrus, had come to the Normandy coast after having met Boudin in Paris. Abandoning genre scenes peopled with figures wearing seventeenth- and eighteenth-century costume, Pécrus lightened his palette and painted scenes of contemporary life. His *Hôtel de la Mer, Trouville*, 1875, is remarkably close in choice of angle to Boudin's *The Beach at Trouville – The Empress Eugénie*, 1863 (pls. 19 and 1). Although Pécrus attempts to create a feeling of the light enveloping the figures and giving the painting an overall harmony, his work lacks the stability, balance and tautness of Boudin. There is a softness, a weakness in his technique, one that Boudin regularly suspected in his own work and fought hard to eradicate.

# 4. Trouville: La Reine des Plages

As we have seen, during the first decades of the nineteenth century artists were attracted to the coastal towns of Normandy by the rugged landscape, the picturesque fishing villages, the sea and, particularly, by the special qualities of the light. At that time, Trouville, situated at the mouth of the navigable river, La Touques, 12 kilometres from Honfleur and 64 kilometres from Le Havre, was a small fishing village with none of the distinguished maritime or military history of Honfleur.

Soon after it had been 'discovered' by the artist Charles Mozin in the 1820s, it became a favoured summer haunt of the artists Isabey, Huet, Corot and Decamps and the novelists and writers Dumas, Karr, Musset and Flaubert. Through their paintings and prints, novels and short stories, Trouville was brought to the notice of a public eager for new leisure pursuits.

The most popular of the summer pursuits was to be the taking of *bains d'eau salée*, the virtues of which had been extolled in the eighteenth century and the popularity of which was to reach a new height during the Second Empire. Along with already established resorts like Dieppe and Boulogne, Trouville became the summer rendezvous of the Parisian aristocracy, thereby earning itself the accolade *la reine des plages*, a title it retained for more than half a century.

The success of Trouville as a summer resort for the elegant and the fashionable was assured when a number of noble families established their summer residences there. Comte Alphonse Napoléon d'Hautpoul (1806–89) and his wife, Caroline Josephine Berthier, daughter of Maréchal Berthier, Prince of Neuchâtel and Wagram, purchased land in Trouville in 1842. Comte d'Hautpoul soon owned extensive property and, through successive periods serving as mayor, played an important role in developing and promoting the resort. Baron Marie-Nicolas Clary and Louise d'Osmond, Comtesse de Boigne (1781–1866), famous as a *salon* hostess, the Duc d'Audiffret-Pasquier (a future President of the National Assembly), the Duc de Maille, descendant of a nephew of Richelieu, and Admiral de Brèze were amongst other members of the aristocracy who, by establishing the 'tone' of Trouville, encouraged the Faubourg Saint-Germain to visit the growing town. As many of these families had, in exile, bathed at Brighton, it is not surprising that they should now wish to do so at Trouville.

By the beginning of the Second Empire the number of inhabitants of Trouville had doubled to 3,504. Summer visitors included the families of businessmen, bankers, industrialists, members of the professions, and many foreigners: Russians, Germans, Belgians and the British. As Trouville became 'less select', the aristocracy, headed by the Duc de Morny, created, on the opposite bank of the river, the rival resort of Deauville, where *le monde* no longer needed to be exposed to or rub shoulders with the *demi-monde* and the *nouveaux riches*.

A manuscript preserved in the archives of the Trouville Museum shows that by June 1838, the anonymous writer was aware of the importance of Trouville beach and its future role in tourism and was keen to promote it: 'The beach is mirror smooth, free from pebbles and silt. These natural advantages have gradually drawn more and more bathers to the place, but although no action was taken at first to make it fashionable, proof had to be given of it; a large number of simple little houses were built. These were remarkably well kept and offered at a modest price accommodation just as suitable as that of most spas. David and the Widow Ozeraie who run the main hotels have enlarged and improved their premises; all manner of suppliers, especially the most essential, have come to set up shop here; a large number of bathing cabins have been built which can be wheeled to the edge of the sea for use as changing rooms. Bathing costumes can be either purchased or hired. A strict policing has recently been introduced to maintain public decency.'[1]

Improvements in transport – numerous stage-coaches and steamers providing a regular service to and from Le Havre, and better roads – and provisions for entertainment, including a casino, allow the writer to conclude that: 'Thanks to these considerable improvements, Trouville, while losing nothing of the charm of its situation, nor of its rustic simplicity, which have previously attracted so many artists and people of good standing, now offers a haven of comforts which the city dweller does not always find it easy to do without.'[2]

Each year saw more villas and hotels built to accommodate the increasing number of visitors attracted to Trouville to partake of the pleasures of the beach and the brilliance of the social life centring around the Casino. As early as 1844, however, some visitors, amongst them Mozin and Flaubert, despaired that the charm of the Trouville they knew was being destroyed: 'Ten years ago, opposite Le Havre and a few leagues from Honfleur, lay the fishing village known as Trouville-sur-Mer. The seascape painters, Isabey and Mozin, used to meet there often and this was where they painted their best studies. Nowhere were the fishing boats more picturesque and the group of cottages which was

20.
Charles Fichot (1817–1903)
Panoramic View of Trouville
1863
Watercolour
Musée de Trouville

Trouville had a truly extraordinary appearance, whether because of the location of the village or because of their extremely primitive design . . . Today Trouville is a fashionable bathing resort. Parisians and many Londoners come here to pitch their tents . . . One day, perhaps, Trouville will be as densely populated as its predecessors; make sure you see it before this happens. The local colour is disappearing, and if you happen upon it, make sure it doesn't get away. Trouville is still picturesque and its cosmopolitan population gives it a very special appearance . . . '[3]

21.

Bathing at Trouville
Photograph
Bibliothèque Nationale, Paris

22.

The Casino at Trouville
Photograph
Bibliothèque Nationale, Paris

23.

The Casino at Trouville
Photograph
Bibliothèque Nationale, Paris

24.

The Hôtel de la Mer, Trouville
Photograph
Bibliothèque Nationale, Paris

# 5. Bains de Mer

*De toutes les fleurs, la fleur humaine est celle qui a le plus besoin de soleil.* Michelet[1]
*Un bain de soleil equivant à un repas'* Dr Gérard[2]

The idea of travelling to the coast for a summer holiday originated in England and was imported to France at the beginning of the nineteenth century. Made possible by the Industrial Revolution, and specifically by the development of the railways, the annual holiday was born. The sea which had previously been seen as a place of work, as a highway or even as a battleground was now recommended for sea-bathing – not, at first, for pleasure but for the good of one's health. Royal and imperial families led the way, soon to be followed by the aristocracy and the bourgeoisie.

As early as the seventeenth century sea-bathing was seen as a cure for rabies. The King's doctor, the Scot Thomas Burnet, in a publication of 1691 stated that 'it is customary to send those who have been bitten by rabid dogs to sea and for them to be immersed 3 times.'[3] In France, Madame de Sévigné told of how the daughters of the Queen, bitten by a rabid dog, were sent to bathe at Dieppe.[4] Not all early bathers, however, were seeking a cure for rabies. The Comtesse de Boigne and Napoleon approved of sea-bathing as did the Duchesse de Berry who, between 1824 and 1830, during visits to Dieppe, bathed each day, wearing 'a scalloped canvas cap secured with straps on her head, a short overcoat, a brown woollen dress trimmed with blue and boots against the crabs'.[5]

There were many publications commending the benefits of sea-bathing and instructing how, when and where one should bathe. In 1660, Dr Wittie of Scarborough in Yorkshire recommended sea-water both for internal and external use. He claimed salt water was good for 'drying up superfluous humours, and preserving from putrefaction; killing all manner of worms'.[6] In 1702 Sir John Floyer and Edward Baynard produced a hefty tome in which they alleged that sea-bathing was useful in the treatment of asthma, cancer, consumption, deafness, rupturism, rheumatism and madness. Further,

> Cold bathing has this good alone;
> It makes old John to hug old Joan!
> And does fresh kindnesses entail
> On a wife tasteless, old and stale.'[7]

Dr Russell's *A Dissertation on the use of sea water in the diseases of the glands*, first published in London in 1752, was translated into French the following year. Bottled sea-water was even available in London because of Russell's claims that it cured everything from colds, consumption and sinus problems to genital ailments.

As the popularity of sea-bathing grew, so did the number of publications on the subject. A marine cure could last for anything from twenty days to two months and was recommended for the treatment of the depressed, the lethargic, the ganglionic; and for those suffering from hypochondria, all persistent nervous diseases, asthma, decay, neurosis and even, but with reservations, consumption and constipation. It was also supposedly excellent in the treatment of sterility. Salt, vegetable and animal matter in the water and iodine in the wind were seen to be the vital ingredients that made sea-bathing so beneficial.

The advice as to when and how to bathe tended to vary from doctor to doctor. Whilst some claimed that the morning was best others recommended bathing between noon and 6 p.m. All unanimously advised waiting some three to four hours after eating a meal. Only one bathe a day was recommended and for a duration of no longer than 15 minutes, to be followed by a hot footbath in sea-water. One writer warned against being inactive in the water, saying the bather should not be content with dipping up and down looking like a monkey or a piston in a steam-engine! Inexperienced bathers held on to the ropes that separated the different areas for bathing. Guides could be hired to accompany the bather and, if necessary, put the bather in the water. Often sailors, these guides can be recognized in paintings by their mode of dress, typically a beret, trousers and shirt. On leaving the water it was advised that the bather should cover up warmly, have a good rub-down, partake of a biscuit and some fortified wine and then, after dressing, walk about half an hour. Most writers mentioned water temperature and only recommended bathing between June and the end of September.

There was further advice available as to the bather's conduct. In his *Des bains de mer. Guide médical et hygiénique du baigneur*, published in 1846, Dr Le Coeur recommended 'great continence in the pleasures of love', while a writer in 1859 claimed that it was 'essential to avoid too much physical exercise, drinking and eating, sensual delight and intellectual effort'.[8] A stay at the seaside was seen, therefore, to be both therapeutic and moral because it assured 'tranquillity of the soul and tranquillity of the spirit.'[9] All in all, it responded to the needs of a changing society.

Coastal dwellers had no doubt been bathing for centuries and almost certainly would have bathed nude. Propriety now dictated that the fashionable ladies frequenting the beaches be protected from improper sights. Rules and regulations were soon drawn up and publicly posted. Gustave Flaubert, who had previously enjoyed bathing at Trouville in the nude, objected to this infringement of his freedom. In a letter to Louise Colet of 14 August 1853 he described how he had 'yesterday spent a good hour watching ladies bathing. What a sight! What a hideous sight!'[10] His feelings were shared by another writer and early bather, Alphonse Karr: 'Women bathing in the sea make the greatest sacrifice to chastity that can be made to any virtue; they sacrifice their beauty to it. With their woollen bathing suits, their jackets, their trousers and their oilcloth bonnets they look like a group of monkeys suffering from ringworm gambolling on the beach. Forced to bathe in the company of men they have had the ingenious idea of surrounding themselves with a veil of ugliness.'[11]

A municipal decree of 1857 permitted bathing in Trouville in three distinct areas. On the right was an area for men only, where *le caleçon simple* was sufficient. To the left there was an area for women and in the centre mixed bathing was permitted to those wearing a full bathing costume where the body was covered from neck to knee. It goes without saying that these areas were strictly guarded.

Throughout the 1850s facilities for those bathing at Trouville were being developed, many under the aegis of the local council which saw such services as a valuable source of revenue. Cabins, either fixed or on wheels, chairs, bathing costumes, robes and towels could be hired by the day, week, fortnight or season. In 1866 the price for hiring a cabin varied from 25 centimes, to 1fr.50 depending on whether you were hiring a *cabine domestique*, a *cabine ordinaire*, a *cabine à flot* or a *cabine de luxe*; towels could be hired for 10 centimes and swimming costumes for 45 centimes while a guide was available for 50 centimes.[12]

The bathing machines pulled by horses were an emblem of the beaches of the nineteenth century and can be seen in a number of Boudin's beach scenes (pls. 32 and 39). They were carefully regulated by the local council. Having purchased a numbered ticket the bather entered the cabin with a door which could be locked by a bolt. Inside there was a bench, a small mirror, a coat-rack or hanger and a wooden tub filled with hot water for rinsing the feet after bathing. A wheeled cabin meant the bather could go straight into the sea right up to the waist, even at low tide.

An important factor in determining the success of a bathing station was accessibility. At the beginning of the nineteenth century good roads, needed for transporting fish, linked Dieppe to the capital but the same was not true of Trouville. Both speculators and the town council quickly recognized the need for road and rail links and encouraged their development.

The railway reached Lisieux in 1855, Pont-l'Evêque by 1858, and Trouville-Deauville in 1863. On Saturday, 3 April 1864, the Duc de Morny, one of the leading developers, himself undertook the journey. The 220 kilometres between the Gare Saint-Lazare and the beach took just over six hours – leaving Paris at 11.25, Morny arrived in Trouville-Deauville at 17.30. By 1873 the journey could be completed in five and a half hours, in four hours in 1882 and in just over three hours in 1913. From the end of the Second Empire to the beginning of the First World War some 150,000 to 175,000 visitors used the Trouville-Deauville station each year.[13]

La Compagnie des chemins de fer de l'ouest offered return tickets, available Saturday to Monday, for 30fr. in 1st class and 22fr. in 2nd. The ordinary tariff was 24fr.60 in 1st, 18fr.50 in 2nd and 13fr.55 in 3rd.[14] Eventually a great variety of fares were offered including returns via Le Havre and season tickets. *Trains de plaisir* were organized, which left Paris very early in the morning and arrived back early the following morning. One such train was laid on in July 1880 for those wishing to attend the Trouville-Deauville regattas.

The guidebooks offered further information on travel. The 1889 Baedeker gives details of the steamer to Le Havre, the omnibus to Honfleur and the prices of cabs: 'With one horse, per drive 1 1/2fr. (luggage included) per hr. 3fr.; with 2 horses 3 and 4fr.; double fare from midnight till 6a.m.'[15]

A great variety of guidebooks were published to help visitors choose between the different bathing stations, early examples including Albert Blanquet's *Guide pittoresque, les bains de mer des côtes normandes*, published by Hachette in 1859 and Emile Tessier's *Guide du touriste en Normandie* of 1861. More general guides included the Guides Joanne, Diamant, Baedeker and Bleu.

In the 1889 English edition of Baedeker's *Northern France*, Trouville beach is described as 'stretching from the harbour to the Hôtel des Roches Noires, a distance of about 2/3m, [it] is one of the finest in France, and during most of the day in the season is thronged with a gay crowd of holiday-makers and bathers in fashionable and attractive costumes. It is bordered for nearly its entire length by a broad paved or boarded promenade, and behind is a row of pleasant villas. It has been epigrammatically described as the 'Summer Boulevard of Paris'.[16]

The description of Trouville beach in Hope-Moncrieff's *Where to Go Abroad*, published in London in 1893, marvellously brings to life the reality behind Boudin's paintings. He begins by quoting the words of others, 'perhaps the most *mondain* bathing-place of France', 'the rendezvous of invalids in good health' and 'a well-aired quarter of Paris recommended by doctors in the months of July and August'. He continues: 'The bathing is on fine sand laid with planks for the convenience of bare feet; and small carriages are used for carrying luxurious bathers down to the edge of the water. Here on hot days revels a carnival of mermaids *à la mode*, who in the most coquettish and not always the most modest of costumes, dive, splash, swim, and paddle themselves about in canoes, mingled with men likewise unconventionally arrayed in stripes and gorgeous hues and draperies of towelling. To the sound of music this spectacle is watched by a crowd at the edge, forming a garden of gay dresses and brilliant sunshades that glow in rivalry with the glaring sand, the white tents, the gigantic fungus-like umbrellas, the green shutters, the striped awnings, the tricoloured flags, and the gilded balconies loaded with flowers in the background. It is certainly a most animated and brilliant sight, especially for connoisseurs in the work of famous man-milliners.'[17]

25.
The Beach at Trouville
*c.*1865–6
Watercolour, 24×43.5cm
Private Collection

# 6. Boudin and Trouville

*Boudin has made the Normandy coastline his speciality. He has even invented a genre of seascapes which is his alone and which consists of painting the beach and all those exotic figures from high society which summer brings to our coastal resorts. They are viewed from a distance but what finesse and liveliness in these figures which, standing or sitting, move on the sand. How good they look in their picturesque surroundings and what a good picture the ensemble creates. The clouds move in the sky, the tide rises, the breeze plays with flounces and skirts. This is the ocean and you can almost smell the salty fragrance.*

Castagnary[1]

Boudin's paintings of the beach at Trouville, particularly those of the 1860s, helped establish his contemporary reputation, brought him some measure of financial security and, in their uniqueness, are what he is largely known for today. Whether it was Boudin himself who first thought of tackling the subject or whether the idea was suggested by his friend Ferdinand Martin or by the example of older artists like Mozin or Isabey is not known. What is certain is that having first visited Trouville in 1861 or 1862 Boudin returned there on a yearly basis throughout the rest of his career.

As Trouville itself grew and developed to meet the needs of a new public, so too did the work of the artist intent on capturing the beauty of the fashionable figures on the beach and the magnificence of the light playing on the sea beyond them. From the beach and jetty scenes of 1862 Boudin went on to explore pictorially the new docks of the growing port, its fishmarket and the washerwomen working on the banks of the river that separated the rival towns of Trouville and Deauville. Eventually, he followed the river Touques further inland and painted a series of landscapes recording the fertile pasture. A few landscapes record the heights of Trouville itself, showing in their style and technique Boudin's awareness and understanding of the works of his younger contemporaries. In the last decade of his life he once more painted the beaches of Trouville and Deauville, and the nearby beaches of Bénerville and Tourgéville. In these broad and airy panoramas fashionable figures and fishermen can still be seen but the figures are now clearly secondary to the true subject of the painting – a celebration of the beauties of nature.

There were aspects of his adopted town that he chose not to explore in paint. Throughout his life Boudin struggled to convey the particular qualities of light, water and air that fascinated him and so it is not surprising that, with few exceptions, he never portrayed the streets, villas and hotels of Trouville.

From Boudin's letters it is clear how much he loved his native Normandy. Keen to travel to find new challenges and new qualities of light, he was always, however, delighted to return to what he considered his home: 'Here we are in Paris. Time to pack our bags and then back to Deauville...yes, indeed! I must admit I am looking forward to seeing our beaches again and our overcast skies.'[2] Enchanted by the task of translating the play of light and the effects of wind and atmosphere on the myriads of figures on the beach at Trouville, he realized that he had found a subject which, by its very nature, provided him with endless variations on the themes most dear to him. Rather than settle in Le Havre or at Honfleur, despite the proximity there in the summer of his artist friends Monet, Jongkind and Dubourg, he chose Trouville.

Although it is hard to be certain, the evidence of letters, notes in his journals and inscriptions on his paintings suggests that every summer, in June or July, Boudin left Paris for Trouville. Sometimes staying only a few nights before travelling on to Brittany, Belgium or Holland, he would, on his return, settle there once more until late October or November. On the rare occasions when he was detained in Paris – as in 1869 when he was completing a commission for the Château de Bourdainville near Rouen – he wrote: 'I dare not think of the beaches bathed in sunshine, of the beautiful stormy skies which it would be so good to paint while breathing the sea air.'[3]

During his early visits to Trouville he stayed in lodgings – at 23 rue Farabe in 1864 and then from 1865 at 9 rue d'Isly. As his financial position became more secure he and Marie-Anne finally decided to build their own home. As it would have been expensive to purchase suitable land in Trouville he chose, in the autumn of 1884, to purchase a plot of land to the extreme west of Deauville near the dunes. The site was selected because of its relatively low price and its quiet aspect and because the road, the rue Oliffe, was perpendicular to the sea. The Villa des Ajoncs or, as Boudin also called it, the Villa Marinette, was gradually extended with the passing years. 'My wife thinks it looks like those little Dutch bird cages in the form of a house and that all that is missing is the ring to hang it from.'[4]

After the death of his beloved wife in 1889 Boudin, lonely and suffering from rheumatism, wrote: ' I have had to leave Deauville because of the cold and because I would die of boredom there in such solitude. But the golden leaves in the gardens still had their pretty smiles.'[5] In his last years, now with the companionship of the new woman who shared his life, Juliette, and the proximity of his favourite views, his home was once more to be a source of comfort and it was to Deauville that he came to spend the last days of his life.

26.

The Beach at Trouville
1863
Oil on canvas, 34.5×57.5cm
Private Collection

# 7. Beach Scenes

*Boudin had invented a genre. He was the first to think of showing formally dressed Parisians, surrounded by air and sun on stretches of beach where the wind is blowing; this was successful and deserved to be.*

Castagnary[1]

*People are starting to ask me for lots of seascapes. I shall do other things but I shall always be the painter of beaches.*

Boudin[2]

Of the eleven paintings that Boudin exhibited at the Paris Salon between 1864 and 1869, nine had Trouville as their subject. Two showed the jetty at Trouville, seven were beach scenes and a tenth painting was of the new Casino at Deauville. Thirty years later, exhibiting at the rival Salon de la Société nationale des beaux-arts, Boudin once again selected paintings of Trouville and Deauville to represent his current oeuvre. From the early paintings of crowds of fashionable figures on the beach or windy jetty, to the late panoramas with only the merest hint of a human presence, we have marvellous evidence of Boudin's development as an artist.

In the beach scenes, the large, highly finished canvases exhibited at the Salon or in the small oil sketches, *pochades*, hastily dashed off to order, we see Boudin's exceptional faculties as an observer and recorder of nature in all its diversity. Although Boudin preferred painting groups of people to painting individuals, he succeeded in capturing the characteristic gestures, movements and costumes of the individual figures with astonishing accuracy. The artistic challenge presented by the subject was not only the representation of movement, colour and light but also the successful incorporation of the human figure into the landscape. With consummate skill Boudin captured glowing skies, sparkling water, and changing atmospheric and weather conditions. At their best, the beach scenes vibrate with subtle nuances of light, colour, shade and movement, tiny and hasty specks of pure colour simultaneously dramatizing the surface and bringing the whole into harmony.

As early as 1863 Boudin saw the potential for commercial success. In a letter to his friend Martin he explained, 'people really like my ladies on beaches, some claim that there is a gold mine there to be exploited'.[3] In a letter written from Paris the following year, he tells Martin that 'our business continues to go well, we shall return with orders to take up part of our summer'.[4] Success, however, was not to be so sudden. In September he writes once more, from Trouville, that he has not 'made a *sou* from our bathers this year. We must just be happy painting them.'[5]

Boudin's letters and journals give a wonderful insight into the artist's mind. A perfectionist, he struggled continually with his technique, never satisfied, always modest. In a letter to the dealer Durand-Ruel he wrote of his doubts: 'I don't know whether you will be satisfied with my new studies. The artist is always disappointed when he brings back his package to the studio.'[6] In addition, Boudin embodies the dilemma faced by an artist striving to earn a living from his art – the choice between painting something that the artist knows will sell or experimenting with style and subject matter and thereby risking losing a known market.

Between 1862 and 1895 Boudin executed more than three hundred paintings, two-thirds of which are dated, showing fashionable holidaymakers on the beaches of Trouville and Deauville. From two dated paintings in 1862, to thirteen in 1863, there is a high point in 1864 with seventeen dated works. He continues to paint an average of ten a year until 1871 after which the numbers fall, with the exception of 1874 and 1880. There are no dated beach scenes in 1876, 1877, 1882, 1883, 1888, 1889, 1890 and 1893. These works do not all have the same degree of finish nor were they intended to have. There is a clear shift in style and in content from the works of the 1860s to the smaller, hastier *pochades* executed from 1867 on, probably at the suggestion of dealers and the insistence of collectors.

Boudin's earliest dated beach scene shows the tiny beach of Honfleur in 1854. Undoubtedly influenced by the masters of Dutch seventeenth-century art and by his own experience, he depicts the local fishermen with their ropes, baskets, rowing boats and beached or anchored fishing boats against a thin line of sand and the sky. This was not a subject he chose to pursue.

It is not known when Boudin first painted in Trouville. The earliest beach scenes executed in oil date from 1862 but, as Boudin's working method consisted of painting outdoors during the summer and finishing the work in the winter in his Paris studio, these paintings were possibly begun in 1861. The essential elements of these compositions are established from the beginning and are then explored with infinite variety in works such as *The Beach at Trouville*, 1863, *The Beach at Trouville*, 1864, and *Beach Scene, Evening*, 1864 (pls. 31, 34, and 33).

A large expanse of sky occupies about two-thirds of the composition with a thin band of sea, often only visible on one side, marking the distant horizon. In the immediate foreground a slightly larger area of sand is empty of incident. In the middle ground, against the low horizon and often placed assymetrically, are the holidaymakers. It is in their rhythmical grouping that Boudin displays his ability to articulate space and his understanding of pictorial harmony. The frieze-like crowd is punctuated by varied groups of standing and seated figures, by children playing on the sands near watchful governesses, by fallen chairs and inquisitive dogs. The space is often further defined by the bathing machines, some on wheels, some being pulled by horses (pl. 39). The cabins, placed at varying angles, lead the viewer's eye around and through the groups. Offering shade from the sun or shelter from the wind, they also provide Boudin with opportunities for dramatic contrasts of light and shade.

These people are all occupied, few sit and dream into space. They chat, gossip or discuss, knit or read, stroll along the sands, and sometimes, though rarely, watch the passing fishing boats, steamers and yachts (pl. 30). Although the *raison d'être* of their visit was bathing in the sea, this aspect of the life of the beach was clearly of little interest to Boudin. With the notable exception of *The Bathing Hour, Trouville*, 1864, there are few examples of actual bathers in his paintings (pl. 37). It is possible, however, that Boudin felt that such a subject would have entailed an unacceptable level of voyeurism.

Except for paintings like *Reunion on the Beach at Trouville*, 1865(Private Collection), intended for the Salon, Boudin's beach scenes are invariably small in scale and painted in oil on panel. Easily portable, the wooden surface also gave added richness and depth of tone and allowed for spontaneity of touch. In his notebooks Boudin frequently mentions the need to work directly from the motif: 'Beaches. Produce them from nature as far as is possible' and 'things done on the spot or based on a very recent impression can be considered as direct paintings. But how many times do we neglect to draw good sketches, true to life sketches on the quaysides, on the beaches and in the streets?'[7] That Boudin did work directly from nature can be seen in tiny unsigned and undated oil studies like *Beach Scene, Trouville* and *Woman with a Parasol on the Beach* (Musée Boudin, Honfleur) which were apparently intended for the artist's own use and were not for sale.

Boudin also worked in pencil and watercolour directly from nature when on the beach. While some of his watercolours were obviously intended as finished works in their own right, others were studies through which he hoped to solve particular compositional problems, or seize and transcribe passing silhouettes, individual figures, groupings and even wind effects before the scene in front of him changed. Boudin favoured watercolour as a means of giving transparency to his compositions and of capturing evanescent light effects. There is a marvellous diversity, charm and spontaneity in his watercolours of the beach at Trouville where he succeeds in giving the impression of expansive space by his use of grey washes or by simply leaving the paper bare.

Some of Boudin's finest beach scenes were painted in 1864 – one of the most magnificent is *Approaching Storm*, where he delights in contrasting the brilliant white of the main figure in the foreground with the looming grey of the threatening sky (pl. 32). Boudin rarely painted particular events, preferring a more intimate view of the beach before him. A brilliant exception is the *Regatta and Fête on the Beach at Trouville*, 1866 (pl. 40). That he had considered this as a possible subject some years earlier is clear from a letter to Martin where he writes that he 'is working with Regattas in mind for the next exhibition'.[8]

From 1867 Boudin's beach scenes appear to have been painted with more haste, no doubt to order rather than from choice. Although some are sketchy in execution, the best are fascinating and repay close attention. In *The Beach at Trouville*, *c.*1870–4, Boudin uses quick, tiny strokes to indicate human activity further down the beach and the small child playing in the foreground is suggested by just a few diagonal strokes of blue and yellow (pl . 41). Although Boudin rarely gives much in the way of facial detail, it is always possible to guess the direction of the glance and the centre of interest of the various holidaymakers even when, as often, they are seen from behind. The sand is enlivened by touches of red and grey and a multitude of tones of brown. In his brushstrokes and paint texture Boudin does not differentiate between his description of the sky, the sand, the sea or the figures – they are all given equal value.

The villas and hotels built along the beach's edge were not of great interest to Boudin who had no particular wish to establish the beach as being that of Trouville rather than any of the other Normandy resorts. The buildings lining the shore are glimpsed in the distance in *Beach Scene*, 1862 (Musée d'Orsay, Paris), but are treated specifically in a small series of paintings executed in 1863. Here, instead of isolating the figures in groups on the beach, Boudin provides them with a distinctive backdrop – the newly developed *quartier des bains*. The key buildings that appear in these paintings are the Casino, Dr Oliffe's house with its distinctive hexagonal tower and the Hôtel de la Mer. Seen from the distance in *The Beach at Trouville*, and from the sea in *The Casino at Trouville*, the

27.
The Beach at Trouville
*c.*1863–5
Pastel, 18.5×27.5cm
Private Collection

clearest view of the buildings is in *The Beach at Trouville* (pls. 29, 28 and 26). In *The Beach at Trouville – The Empress Eugénie*, he has moved round still further and all that can now be made out is the main façade of the hotel, the terrace of the Casino and the marquee in front of it (pl. 1).

It would have been surprising if Boudin had never painted this area as it was the bathers' social centre. It was not sufficient for the developing resort to attract a distinguished clientele, it also had to provide meeting places and entertainment to keep the visitors occupied. A clear mark of the prosperity of any resort was the presence of a

casino, a source of lucrative revenue that made possible the financing of grand and varied entertainments for the holidaymakers.

In Trouville, the history of gaming began in 1837, when Valle, one of the founders of the new resort, bought a plot of land beside the beach for the sum of 650 francs and erected the first Salon des Bains. This Salon, essentially a rendezvous for families of the aristocracy, was a simple square pavilion. For an entrance price of 10 francs per person for the season the visitor, as well as having access to the gaming tables, had the use of the changing-room, the small library – containing 500 novels and 4 journals – and a room providing shelter from the sun or the rain.[9]

Interesting details of the early days of the Casino are furnished by a manuscipt in the archives of the Trouville Museum. Written in 1838 it records that the Casino's library

28.

The Casino at Trouville
1863
Oil on panel, 23×43cm
Private Collection

29.
The Beach at Trouville
1863
Oil on canvas, 43×72cm
Private Collection. Courtesy of
Galerie Schmit, Paris

included novels by Walter Scott, George Sand and Balzac and that the Casino was open and lit until 11p.m. – 'subscription balls could be given there; there would be lighting and an orchestra at not too great an expense'.[10] The manuscript continues: 'People gather there for parties and concerts. It also has its faithful whist, écarté and billiards fans. But there is always a great concern about appearance and setting the right tone. Frock coats and crinolines compete in terms of elegance and sophistication.'[11]

This first building was soon replaced by the Casino to be seen in Boudin's paintings. In September 1844 Dr Oliffe bought a plot of land facing the sea with access to what would soon be the rue de la Plage. This land belonged to David, the owner of the L'Agneau d'Or, and to the architect Breney. In 1851 Dr Oliffe formed a Société du Casino-Salon to last for a period of thirty years. In 1881, at its liquidation, the shares

originally purchased for 500 francs were worth 6,000 francs. The shareholders, presided over by A. Cordier, included the Comtesse de Balleroy, the Comte d'Hautpoul and the Duc d'Audiffet-Pasquier.

In 1851, the Casino-Salon consisted of a ground floor opening over the rue de la Plage with a raised rotunda and terrace looking over the beach. 'Tucked away on one side in a narrow street this salon is a little monument on the sea which grew year by year under the capable guidance of its architect, Breney. It looks like a railway station built at the edge of the water, which sweeps past with considerable force in the equinoxes. People play whist and *bouillotte* there, read newspapers and magazines, dance the lancers and the mazurka in those beautiful galleries timbered with northern pine where the

30.
The Beach at Trouville
1863
Oil on panel, 34.9×57.8cm
The National Gallery of Art, Washington;
Collection of Mr & Mrs Paul Mellon

31.
The Beach at Trouville
1863
Oil on panel, 26×48cm
Private Collection

most illustrious Parisian artists come to give concerts.'[12]

On hot and sunny days as many as 400 members could sit outside on the canopied terrace and watch the animated spectacle of the beach, the passing steamers and fishing boats. Inside, the Casino had ' ball-rooms, concert-rooms, card-rooms, private club-rooms, and a theatre. Theatrical performances take place twice a week, and a grand ball is usually given on Sundays.'[13] 'Gambling is one of the main attractions of the casino at Trouville. Often play is for very high stakes, especially when the races are on or when gentlemen who have lost come to try to win back their fortunes. A few years ago the Trouville salon was modest and peaceful. Duke Pasquier and Rossini played their game of cards in silence; at that time the curfew was sounded at 11 o'clock . . . [today] all kinds

of foolishness enliven the casino's salons every evening until midnight and often until three and four in the morning.'[14]

The Baedeker for 1889 provides further details on the price of admission to the Casino: 'Admission for one day 2fr. (bet. July 16 and Sept 16 = 3fr.); per fortnight, for 1 person 30fr., 2 pers = 50fr.; per month, 40 and 60fr.; per half season (July 1st to Aug 10, or Aug 10 to close) 50 and 75fr.;3 months 60 and 100fr.'[15]

In the early years frequent visitors included Dr Oliffe, the Duc and Duchesse de Morny, the Princesse de Metternich, the Comtesse de Pourtales, the Marquise de Gallifet and the Duchesse de la Tremoille.[16] In the 1884 edition of Baedeker, the Casino is

32.
Approaching Storm
1864
Oil on panel, 36.6×57.9cm
The Art Institute of Chicago, Mr & Mrs L. L. Coburn Memorial Collection

33.
Beach Scene, Evening
1864
Oil on panel, 36×58cm
Alex. Reid and Lefevre, London

described as offering 'all the appropriate resources for this sort of establishment and it is exceedingly refined.'[17] An English writer in 1893 relates how for 'entrance to the Casino apartments themselves, there is some attempt at examination of social qualifications, but this sifting process does not seem to be a very rigorous one. Money is the main "Open Sesame" of Trouville . . . the subscribers certainly get enough in the way of balls, spectacles, plays, and whatsoever amusements are in vogue.'[18]

The flags fluttering in the breeze and the white marquee pinpoint the Casino in *The Beach at Trouville – The Empress Eugénie* (pl. 1). Although there is no documentary evidence to prove that the painting shows the Empress and the ladies of the court there is

no reason to doubt the traditional title. The originality of Boudin's treatment of the subject and the strong light highlighting the figure in white suggest that the small panel commemorates a visit by the Empress to the fashionable resort. The Empress loved travelling both on official journeys which consisted of balls, banquets and the theatre and, as here, incognito. Trouville was frequented by other members of the court including the Princesse de Metternich, the Comtesse de Pourtales and the Duc de Morny, who was half-brother and adviser to the Empress's husband Napoleon III.

An historian of the period describes how the Second Empire, 'like the reign of Louis XV, was an era of adoration of the female of the species; she played a vital role in society, provoked marvellous ingenuity in the creators of fashion and manufacturers of cosmetics and demanded higher and higher living standards'.[19] Eugénie de Montijo

34.
The Beach at Trouville
1864
Oil on panel, 27.7×47.5cm
Richard Green Gallery, London

35.
Beach Scene
1866
Watercolour and pencil, 14.5×26.7cm
Département des Arts Graphiques, Louvre

36.
Beach Scene
1866
Watercolour and pencil, 14.5×26.8cm
Département des Arts Graphiques, Louvre

(1826–1919) was admired for her great beauty: in 'the sixties, the Empress was still very beautiful. Her delicate colouring, the shape of her head, her golden-blonde hair, the expression of her mouth, her beautiful shoulders, and the grace of her movements were as enchanting as ever.'[20] Until the sudden death of her sister in 1860 the Empress loved blue but from this time on she preferred subdued colours, wearing gowns of pearly grey, ash grey, black or white.

Behind the promenading group is the Hôtel de la Mer which can be seen more clearly in a contemporary photograph (pl. 24). The hotel was formed out of one of the twin houses built for Dr Oliffe and the architect M. Breney in 1845. The Hôtel and the near-

37.
The Bathing Hour, Trouville
1864, Oil on canvas, 41×65cm
Private Collection. Courtesy of Galerie Schmit, Paris

38.
Beach Scene, Trouville
*c.*1865–7, Oil on cardboard, 22.5×29cm
Musée Eugène Boudin, Honfleur

39.
Bathing Time at Deauville
1865
Oil on panel, 34.5×57.9cm
The National Gallery of Art, Washington; Collection of Mr & Mrs Paul Mellon

by Casino-Salon were demolished in the 1930s to make way for the Palais Normand.

The Hôtel de la Mer was established in 1855 at a time when more hotels, especially with a view of the sea, were needed. Years before, when Dumas and Mozin had visited, there were only two rather basic inns, the Auberge de Bras d'Or of Mère Ozeraie and L'Hôtel de l'Agneau d'Or managed by the David family. In the 1850s lodgings were still remarkably cheap, 40 sous for board and lodging for painters and 50 sous for everyone else.

The first reasonably comfortable hotel, built in 1840, was L'Hôtel de la Plage, later renamed L'Hôtel de Paris, just out of the painting to the left in *The Casino at Trouville* (pl.

40.

Regatta and Fête on the Beach at Trouville
1866
Oil on canvas, 41×64cm
Private Collection, Germany

28). Apart from dining-rooms and bedrooms, it also had a billiard room, a ballroom, a gymnasium and a games room. By the turn of the century this hotel had 200 rooms with bathrooms and 30 apartments, and *belle époque* visitors included Sarah Bernhardt and the Rothschilds.[21]

Another early hotel can be glimpsed in some of Boudin's paintings of Trouville port (pl. 61). The distinctive white building on the place de la Cahotte is the Hôtel Bellevue, opened in 1843. Comprising four floors, it was the tallest building in Trouville. The hotel's second owner was the Parisian music publisher Schlesinger whose wife Elisa was the muse of Flaubert's first novels. Another important hotel, the Hôtel des Roches

Noires, celebrated in Monet's painting of 1870 (Musée d'Orsay, Paris), attracted aristocrats, financiers, millionaires and dandies.

Boudin's early beach scenes are regarded today as amongst his finest creations but he did not find them easy to paint. A perfectionist, he continually struggled to improve his technique. On 7 April 1863, he recorded a conversation he had had with the artist Troyon and from the context it is clear that they had discussed Boudin's beach scenes. Troyon evidently believed that Boudin had been searching for the wrong things. Boudin, with some reservations, agreed. 'My painting has become dull because the figures are lifeless, lack definition, convey no sense of movement. I must return to my original method which may have been more rigid but paid more attention to form. Follow Van de Velde's example and emphasize the sky, put more energy into it.' He continues: 'A bright or silvery white, yet with depth, substance, clarity of touch and line; underneath it, a small well-placed figure, secondary to the vast sky – power and clarity. If I could render that image as I see it today, I would not be ashamed of the result. Sometimes a diabolic energy in the vivid effects and depth and mystery in the pale infinities.'[22]

That he was still concerned about this can be seen from his comments after visiting the Salon of 1864 where his *Beach near Trouville* (private collection) was exhibited. 'First

41.

The Beach at Trouville
*c.*1870–4
Oil on panel, 20×46cm
The National Gallery, London

42.

Trouville, Low Tide
1872
Oil on canvas, 66×95cm
Private Collection. Courtesy of Galerie Schmit, Paris

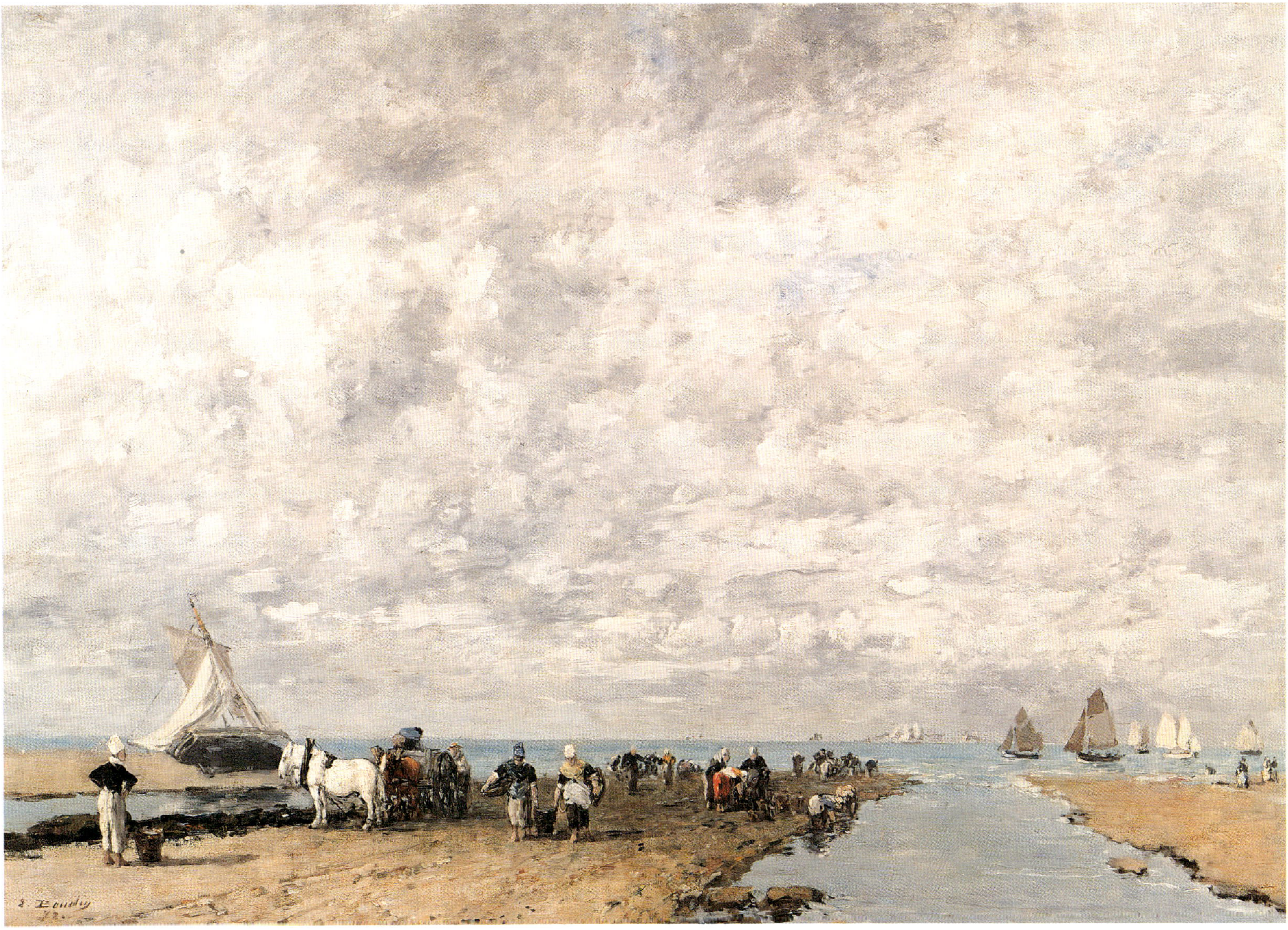

visit. Observe that the backgrounds have a warm tone and are less hard than I see them.'[23] He then resolves to try and put 'more warmth, brightness and forcefulness into my paintings. Look for the most striking contrasts in costumes. Concentrate on drawing. Also attempt the superb effects of a sky with something almost inconspicuous on the sea or on the beach. Closely observe the whole and tackle it energetically on all fronts. Try for flatness in the modelling but intense tonality. Exaggerate one element to make it stand out. Make special studies of boats and equipment. Fresh and vivid – nothing patchy.'[24]

The following year he is again dissatisfied with his paintings *Deauville Casino* (Na-

43.
Shrimp Fishers at Trouville
1879
Oil on canvas, 22×42cm
Private Collection, Courtesy of
Galerie Schmit, Paris

44.
The Sand Dunes at Tourgéville
1890
Oil on canvas, 55×88cm
Private Collection

tional Gallery, Washington) and *Trouville Beach – Bathing Hour* (Toledo Museum of Art, Ohio). Leaving the exhibition he despairs: 'too blue, too blue. More space in the groups, figures smaller. More balance. Think out the painting in advance and ponder it well. Try grey effects but with a warmer appearance.'[25] In a letter to his brother Louis, he complains that the work 'does not give an idea of what I have achieved in smaller paintings. Bothered by the size of the figures which I had to do without a model, I failed.'[26] He knows what he is searching for but fears he will not succeed: 'these delicate skies and beaches. Attempt to convey the sheen of my subjects or the very essence of the water, misty backgrounds, delicate figures. All that takes time, however, and we poor beggars,

pushed forward far too quickly, have little time for individual items.'[27]

That Boudin had a love-hate relationship with his beach scenes is obvious from a number of letters written in the period 1867-8. In a letter to Ferdinand Martin of 28 August 1867 on his return from Normandy he describes how the 'beach at Trouville, which a little while ago delighted us, looks on my return just like a terrible masquerade . . . You practically need to be a genius to turn this troop of lazy "posers" to good account. When you have just spent a month among people doomed to the hard labour of the fields, black bread and water and find yourself confronted with this troop of golden

45.
A Beach near Trouville
1890
Oil on canvas, 45×75.5cm
Graves Art Gallery, Sheffield

46.
The Beach at Deauville, Low Tide
1893
Oil on canvas, 50.8×103.2cm
Courtauld Institute Galleries, University of London; Courtauld Bequest

parasites who look so triumphant, it inspires a little pity in you and a certain shame in painting idle laziness. Fortunately, dear friend, the Creator spread a little of his splendid warming light everywhere and it is less these people than the element surrounding them which we are reproducing. But Bihama is so much more beautiful than these ladies in satin with her white canvas skirt, her red and black blouse and her long hair when she shakes her basket at the water's edge and the grain falls thick and pure on the sailcloth. And those who beat husks in the golden dust of rye and barley, and those who pray, kneeling on the granite flagstones of the church, which has no chairs.'[28]

It is surely no coincidence that 1867 was the last year in which Boudin worked seriously on these beach scenes, his later paintings being slighter in both content and technique. His decreasing interest in the subject did not mean, however, that he would accept criticism of his beach scenes without defending himself. Boudin was aware that their success contained an element of danger, for while continually striving after perfection, he knew he still had to meet the incessant demands of collectors and dealers who imposed limited time-scales. Ferdinand Martin believed Boudin to be in danger of los-

47.
The Beach at Trouville
1895
Oil on canvas, 54.3×81.2cm
The Barber Institute of Fine Arts, University of Birmingham

ing his artistic integrity, and accused him of pandering to the taste of the bourgeois buying public in literally 'churning out' such scenes. In 1868 Martin wrote to Boudin asking 'very seriously to put your Trouville beaches aside for a moment and return to your seascapes'.[29]

On 3 September 1868, Boudin was spurred into a passionate defence of his art and his subject matter. Martin's letter arrived as he was showing some of his artist friends, including Ribot, 'my little studies of fashionable beaches. These gentlemen congratulated me specifically for daring to paint contemporary people and objects, for finding a way of making the man in an overcoat and the lady in waterproofs acceptable by means of the form and presentation.' Boudin pointed out that the Italians and Flemish had painted scenes of contemporary life and in his own day Millet had chosen to paint the life of the peasant. Boudin argued, 'these middle-class people walking on the jetty towards the sunset – have they no right to be set on canvas, to be brought to the light? Between you and me they are often seeking rest after working hard in their offices. There may be a few parasites among them, but they are also people who have done their jobs. That is a genuine, irrefutable argument.

'I would not wish to condemn myself to painting daubs under any circumstances but isn't it pathetic to see serious people such as Isabey, Meissonier and so many others

48.
A Beach near Trouville
Pastel, 25.4×39.4cm
The Bowes Museum, Barnard Castle

49.
The Beach at Trouville
1883
Pencil, 11.6×15.5cm
Département des Arts Graphiques, Louvre

searching out gaudy carnival clothes and because it is supposed to be picturesque using them on models, who as often as not do not know how to carry off borrowed finery.

'I allowed myself this digression, my dear chap, because you are misled by your friendship: you are worried about me and you think that I should take a step backwards and make concessions to the tastes of certain people. I was unhappy for a long time and was therefore worried enough to have delved, searched, thought. I have sounded out others enough to know their abilities and then I weigh mine. And, my dear friend, I continue along my little path, even though it is very narrow, my only wish being to walk more confidently, widening the path a little when necessary. You can find art in anything if you are gifted. Anyone who holds a paintbrush or a pen must believe they are gifted. It is up to the public to judge and up to the artist to move forward and to capture nature, whether it is by painting cabbages, cheeses or supernatural and divine beings. So I do not accept your opinion that I choose my subjects badly: on the contrary I am becoming more and more attached to them, hoping to expand this genre which is still too limited.'[30]

Whether as a result of Martin's stinging comments, a changing market or the artist's own interests, Boudin did not paint any really important beach scenes after 1867. Although he continued to paint small beach scenes with fashionable figures until the last years of his life, there is no feeling that he was deliberately exploring new territory.

Boudin was never tempted to paint the fashionable beaches of any of the other seaside resorts such as Dieppe. Although he did paint beach scenes elsewhere, particularly at Berck and Kerhor, his interests there were quite different. His experiences, however, especially at Berck, suggested another subject for exploration. *Trouville, Low Tide*, 1872, is one of the most magnificent of Boudin's paintings showing fishermen and washerwomen at work on the beach, near the narrow channel of the river Touques (pl. 42). The subject matter is similar to that found in the works of Dutch artists of both the seventeenth and the nineteenth century, and Boudin depicts a beached fishing boat, horses and cart, and the men busy with their load. The women with their heavy baskets, some of whom can be seen kneeling beside the water, are probably washerwomen.

*Shrimp Fishers at Trouville*, 1879, is a variant of a composition Boudin was to return to on numerous occasions (pl. 43). Since 1830 the women of Trouville, when their men were at sea, were documented as having fished when the tide was out, thereby supplementing their low incomes. Although in this painting it is only locals who can be seen fishing with nets for shrimps, other works show the fashionable holidaymakers participating. One early guidebook advises the visitor to buy the net used by the locals for 'the shrimp fishing is good and full of surprises because you can also catch many small coastal fish which like to hide in the sand and approach the shore in summer'.[31] Fishing is described in another early guidebook as 'another popular amusement, and the gathering of mussels or oysters among the rocks and shallows, which at least makes an excuse for fine ladies to wade about and show their ankles in short skirts after the fisherwomen fashion. Both the coast and the river are rich in fish.'[32]

During the last decade of his life Boudin executed a superb series of large canvases of panoramic views of the beaches of Trouville and Deauville and others in the immediate vicinity. Unlike his earlier paintings these are almost empty of human figures. In *The Beach at Deauville, Low Tide*, 1893, local fishermen work beside the horses and cart in the foreground, while the visitors, mere flecks of paint, promenade in the distance (pl. 46). In these later works the paint is thinly applied, the darker areas of the clouds suggested by the brown ground of the canvas which Boudin allows to show through. In the foreground thin brown lines heighten the feeling of pictorial depth and add a feeling of rushing movement. Similar lines can be seen in *The Beach at Trouville*, 1895, the artist

50.
The Beach at Trouville
*c.*1865–9
Pencil, 10×20.6cm
Département des Arts Graphiques, Louvre

having moved further out from the town itself to the cliffs beside the black rocks (pl. 47). The remoteness and tranquillity of the scene are emphasized by the inclusion of the lone figure of a fisherwoman.

That Boudin did not entirely abandon his interest in the holidaymakers in these late paintings can be seen in the glorious *A Beach near Trouville*, 1890, and in a pastel of the same subject (pls. 45 and 48). A couple walk towards us, some children play in a rock pool, other figures are hastily sketched in. Boudin's real interest, however, is in capturing the broad expanse of beach and sky and in suggesting the freshness of the air. In the same year, in *The Sand Dunes at Tourgéville*, Boudin, influenced by earlier paintings he had executed at Berck, is as interested in the landscape behind the beach as in the beach itself (pl. 44). Throughout, however, even if the particular focus of his interest shifts, his aim is the same, to capture the marvellous beauty of nature in a harmonious whole. 'Sometimes when I'm out walking, in a melancholy frame of mind, I look at this light which floods the earth, which quivers on the water and plays on clothes and it is frightening to think how much genius is required to capture so many difficulties, how limited man's spirit is, not being able to put all these things together in his head. And then again I sense that the poetry is there and sense how to capture it. I sometimes catch a glimpse of what would have to be expressed.'[33]

# 8. Jetties

*You may feel that Boudin's seascapes,* The Jetty at Le Havre *and* Setting off for the Pardon, *are not sufficiently finished, that the drawing is a little careless? You are right if you look at them up close, but not otherwise. How fine and true the tone, how lively and active all those little figures are in the surrounding air. These are effects constantly seen on our Normandy coasts. Nothing is felt as vividly or portrayed as colourfully; and it is also original. Boudin is the only person who approaches seascapes in this way or, as Courbet, who put it so much better, says 'He has carved himself a charming little niche with the* paysage de mer *from which no one will dislodge him.'*

Castagnary[1]

With the exception of a few early works showing the jetty at Honfleur, the only scenes of jetties that Boudin painted were those of Trouville-Deauville. Originally constructed in the period 1840–50 as the result of a subscription launched by the sailors of Trouville, they were lengthened in 1858–9. The purpose of the two jetties was to shorten and deepen the narrow channel leading in to the port. These distinctive jetties, close to and accessible from the beach, became part of the ritual promenade of Trouville's visitors. Here, especially on windy days, the visitors much enjoyed watching as the fishing boats, the Le Havre steamer and three-masted vessels fought against the swell and attempted to navigate the narrow channel.

Unlike the masters of Dutch seventeenth-century art, or contemporaries such as Monet, Boudin rarely painted ships out at sea (pl. 59). Although in Boudin's paintings, quays, docks and dockyards might seem to be of secondary importance, they in fact provide a convenient structure by means of which the artist defines pictorial space. In the distinctive Trouville-Deauville jetties Boudin found an appropriate compositional device which he was to use in more than 220 paintings.

These paintings fall into three distinct types: 7 paintings of the jetty at Trouville painted between 1862 and 1869; 200 works showing both jetties at high or low tide, from 1876 on; and 6 paintings of Deauville jetty from the late 1880s and 1890s.

*The Jetty at Trouville*, 1869, is a magnificent example of the first and earliest type (pl. 54). On canvas and, by Boudin's standards, large in scale, it reproduces, with only minor changes, the composition of two paintings he exhibited at the Salons of 1867 and 1868. In repeating such a subject, and on such a scale, it is likely that the painter was responding to a specific commission from a collector who had seen the earlier works. It is interesting to note that both of the paintings exhibited in the Salon have in the Boudin literature been wrongly entitled *The Jetty at Le Havre*. From Boudin's own notebooks we know that the painting exhibited in 1867 as *The Jetty* was in fact that of Trouville. The 1868 painting appeared in the Salon catalogue and, as can be seen from the Castagnary quote above, was even reviewed as being *The Jetty at Le Havre*. Comparison of the three works, the evidence of the notebook, and the inscription on the Burrell Collection painting prove beyond doubt, however, that all three are of the jetty at Trouville.

These early paintings can be seen as an extension of Boudin's beach scenes begun in the same year, 1862. In *The Jetty at Trouville*, against a vast expanse of cloudy sky and a low horizon, groups of fashionably dressed figures chat, hang on to their hats, walk or watch the fishing boats heading out to sea. The two figures seated on a bench near the lamp-post on the extreme right of the composition help lead the viewer into the painting. As in the beach scenes, most of the figures are seen from behind, with the exception of the man walking towards us in the middle foreground, who looks extremely cold. His obvious discomfort is heightened by his gesture – holding his coat to his face – and by the fact that Boudin has not tried to suggest the roundness of his form, choosing instead to convey the feeling of the man being literally flattened by the wind.

Boudin delights in suggesting the contrasting textures of the silk dresses, the hard quayside, the foaming, frothy, wind-swept waves and the softer clouds. He enjoys playing with the light on the sails, contrasting the deep shadow of the sail of the vessel closest to us with the light striking the sails of those further out to sea. The diagonal line of the Deauville jetty on the extreme left echoes the direction of the boats and gives an impression of depth, an effect opposed by the frieze-like line of figures to the right. The strong notes of blue, green, red and yellow bring the predominantly grey-blue tonality to life. The small brushstrokes and areas of rich impasto enliven the painting's surface and make a harmony of the whole. As Boudin was continually reminding himself, 'The main thing is that the colours and harmony work.'[2]

A painting such as this eloquently demonstrates Boudin's mastery and thorough understanding of how a boat actually sits in the water – a fact continually commented upon by his contemporaries. Such knowledge involved much patient observation, as Boudin explained to Martin: 'if you saw my studies, in spite of their lack of finish, but what a lot of problems . . . you see a boat sailing past, which you hardly have time to capture, and

51.
Paul Helleu
Boudin Working
Drypoint
The National Gallery of Scotland, Edinburgh

52.
Charles Mozin
The Jetty at Trouville
Lithograph
Musée de Trouville

the water, its waves disturbed by the wind or the steamer'.[3] And in his notebook: 'Seascapes. The same research. Do not paint them until you have found what is striking and true about them . . . Do not be afraid of the great effects in the sky and on the sea, tackle their diversity and power without worrying about convention.'[4] The weather, which could be a source of great joy, could equally cause Boudin much sorrow: 'In short, summer has not been kind to us: hardly any reasonable days . . . and it was hardly painters' weather, a blue sky [illegible] completely blue with no effects . . . '[5]

There was great commercial potential for Boudin's seascapes, a fact noted by Monet as early as June 1859: 'there is a complete lack of seascape artists and it is a path which could take you far'.[6] In a letter to Martin, written in December 1869, Boudin lists the various dealers and collectors who have been to see him: 'Hagerman, the art dealer I mentioned to you, discovered my collection of seascapes and bought them on the spot. He would have liked to buy all of them but I kept a few back for Mr Martin who also bought a batch. Tomorrow I am expecting the Belgian, Mr Gauchez, and another customer who also wants boats. So, inevitably, I have returned to being a seascape artist. How strange.' Once more Boudin is quick to point out to Martin: 'Don't think that this is making me neglect the artistic side of things. On the contrary, I feel more than ever the need to be strict with myself and to seek this perfection which we all pursue as far as our skills allow. That is why without worrying about the low prices I am paid I strive to do better and better. We have to contend with talented fellows.'[7]

Given the success of his early seascapes it is not known why Boudin should have abandoned painting works like *The Jetty at Trouville* after 1869. It is entirely possible, however, that collectors wanted beach scenes with fashionable figures or shipping scenes, but not paintings that included both. It was only eight years later, in 1876, that Boudin returned once more to painting the jetties.

In 200 paintings, superficially repetitive but each essentially different, he shows the jetties at high or low tide. Most are small in scale, executed on panel and were certainly started, if not finished, on the spot. The works of horizontal format usually include both jetties which, advancing towards the low horizon and a vanishing point, help define the stage for the action. At high tide fishing boats prepare to set sail, or return to port, their masts and billowing sails contrasting with the strong horizontals of the jetties. Tiny figures can be made out pulling ropes and, in the background, small and hasty flecks of paint suggest distant figures. The light triangle of the central sails in *Trouville, The Jetties at High Tide*, 1890, and their reflection in the water provide the central motif of the

53.
The Jetty at Trouville
Photograph
Bibliothèque Nationale, Paris

54.
The Jetty at Trouville
1869
Oil on canvas, 64.8×92.8cm
Glasgow Museums: The Burrell Collection

painting and its visual focus (pl. 57). In *Trouville, The Jetties at Low Tide*, *c.*1885–90, we again see how Boudin is content to empty his painting of incident and, in juxtaposing similar shapes and blocks of colour, take as his subject something that is essentially abstract (pl. 56).

Three-quarters of these paintings show the jetties at low tide, as in *Trouville, The Jetties at Low Tide*, 1888 (pl. 55). Was this because Boudin found this subject more appealing or because, with the boats beached, the only movement he needed to capture

was that of the clouds in the sky and their reflection in the shallow water? From the evidence of the dated paintings, from Paul Helleu's print of *Boudin Working* and a late photograph of the artist, we know that Boudin continued to paint scenes such as this, outside and from nature, until the end of his life.

55.
Trouville, The Jetties at Low Tide
1888, Oil on canvas, 32.5×41cm
The National Gallery, London

56.
Trouville, The Jetties at Low Tide
*c.*1885–90
Oil on panel, 26.3×21.3cm
Glasgow Museums: The Burrell Collection

57.
Trouville, The Jetties at High Tide
1890
Oil on panel, 31×42cm
Private Collection

58.
The Shore near Trouville
*c.*1883–7
Oil on panel, 28×40.6cm
Perth Museum and Art Gallery

59.
The Shore at Deauville
1891, Oil on panel, 37.4×46.3cm
Glasgow Museums: Art Gallery and Museum, Kelvingrove

# 9. The Port

*Nearly 20 years ago, if not more, Boudin, this simple, honest, wise and profound observer started to paint ports, fishermen, the endlessly changing skies over the Channel, Parisians bathing in the sea. From then on the modern sea, complete with fishermen, small boats, ports, Parisians on the jetties or near the bathing cabins, suddenly interested painters who before were familiar only with shipwrecks, storms, attacks and fires – the dramas and melodramas of the sea.*

Duranty[1]

As we have seen, Boudin was fascinated by the world of the sea, a world he loved and with which he felt at ease. From his earliest years in Honfleur and Le Havre until his last days in Deauville, the busy, ever-changing life of the ports presented him with a subject of infinite variety.

First at Honfleur, then at Le Havre in the late 1850s, he documented his home ports but, unlike earlier artists such as Gagnery or Leprince, or contemporaries such as Hamelin, Boudin avoided the life of the quayside with the unloading of fish and the embarkation or disembarkation of passengers. Instead he concentrated on the ships, entering or leaving the harbour, at all times of day and night. Three-masted ships, steamers, yachts and fishing boats are seen together, or in solitary majesty. Even after he established his summer home in Trouville, Boudin continued to paint the larger and more active port of Le Havre.

The coastal ports and natural harbours of Brittany also attracted him as early as 1855, the main period of his activity being in the 1870s. The emphasis was on the fishermen and women, as they waited on the beach for the returning boats, their horses and carts at the ready to unload the fish, a subject he never depicted at Trouville. Whether at Portrieux, Quimper or Camaret, Boudin evolved a particular type of composition specific to each place, which he then explored and developed during later visits.

Boudin worked elsewhere in the north of France including Dunkerque, Fécamp, Berck, Etaples, Etretat, Abbeville and Dieppe. He also worked at Bordeaux, though he did try to distance himself from the working area of the port which, in a letter to Martin of February 1875, he described as far too noisy. The milling crowds of workers, waiting carts, the forest of masts might delight someone in search of activity but 'that does nothing for the dreamer who prefers a little silence and solitude, the duller but more poetic tones of natural elements'. In Bordeaux Boudin missed 'the seaweed and . . . the fresh salt air of our shores'.[2]

When Boudin travelled abroad, to Holland and Belgium, to Rotterdam, Dordrecht, Brussels and Anvers, and later to Venice, he chose to stay in towns or cities with busy, active and distinctive ports. At the end of his life, in the south of France, he portrayed the natural harbour of Villefranche. His depth of knowledge and achievement were summarized by the critic Gustave Geffroy, who, in a review written in 1883, wrote that: 'In love with the sea whatever the time of day or year, he has stopped everywhere and noted the different aspects of the same landscape. He knows all the inlets, all the ports, all the river mouths. He paints life and solitude; the dramas occurring between the stones and the water interest him as much as the goings-on in a coastal town. He records alluvial formations, the pools of water left far inland by high tides; he also records docks cluttered with high-sided vessels. He is full of the poetry of the sea and he is wholly familiar with the technique of navigation.'[3]

By comparison with the ports that Boudin painted elsewhere in France, the port of Trouville was small and quiet. He set out to explore it during his first stay in Trouville when he was painting his first scenes of the beach and jetties. Boudin painted the port of Trouville throughout his career, changing his viewpoint as the port itself developed, growing steadily busier with trade, fishing boats and the yachts of the wealthier visitors.

Until the middle of the nineteenth century, it was the small port of Touques that served the river Touques which entered the English Channel at the mouth of the Seine. During the period 1840–65, with the gradual development of the port of Trouville, the importance of Touques diminished and by the 1870s few ships travelled up-river to the old port. A map of 1829 shows the river Touques flowing almost straight out past Trouville. On the right bank some fishermen's houses and two quays – Quai de la Cahotte and Quai de la Poissonnerie – are indicated. The left bank, where Deauville now stands, was only a marshy plain, with some small islands and sandbanks. These first quays – known as Les Ecores and commemorated in a large painting by Isabey – were no more than a rough sea-wall continually battered by the changing tides. In spate, the river frequently displaced the boulders which then damaged the hulls of boats moving up-river to Touques.

The impetus for the new port came when a road, constructed along the quayside, caused the right bank of the river to be straightened and services such as sanitation,

60.
Trouville Harbour
*c*.1877–81
Oil on canvas, 37×55cm
Manchester City Art Gallery

water and public lighting to be introduced. The Comte d'Hautpoul, elected mayor in 1845, was responsible for initiating, and largely funding, many of these modernization projects. As the small port was still at the mercy of the changing tides, a channel was dredged out beside the Pointe de la Cahotte to regularize the currents and water-level, being completed by 1849. The construction of the jetties in the period 1840-50 further aided the navigation of this channel.

By 1846 the façade of the town and the quays were realigned. Two wider areas were also developed: one at the rue des Bains allowing for the construction of the fishmarket in 1844; the other for the boatyard which until 1867 had been situated on the Pointe de la Cahotte. The port was officially inaugurated on 5 April 1849 but development continued with the construction of a floating dock on the left bank, entered by a lock. The brainchild of the Duc de Morny, the dock cost 2,400,000 francs of which 300,000 francs were furnished by Donon and Oliffe. The dock was inaugurated on 10 April 1866 in the presence of Breney, Hautpoul, Oliffe and a large crowd, but without the Duc de Morny who had died in March 1865. Another dock was built in 1890 and can be seen in *The Lock at Trouville*, 1894 (pl. 67).

The larger ships were berthed in the Bassin Morny and it is this dock that can be seen in many of Boudin's paintings such as *Deauville, The Dock*, 1888, and that of 1891 (pls. 65 and 66). These small oils, like those of the jetties, are celebrations of the ships themselves and not of the activity in the port.

For much of the nineteenth century, fishing was the principal industry in Trouville. In the 1870s there were 75 large fishing boats from 25 to 35 tons and smaller vessels of 3 to 8 tons which between them employed 700–800 fishermen. As the port grew and the docks were opened trade also grew with wood from the north, English coal and cement being imported and cider and hay exported.

The course of the river was changed when an outer harbour was constructed beside the Pointe de la Cahotte. The river could be crossed here by ferry or, depending on the tide, by a wooden footbridge. Here too was sited the landing stage for the steamships from Le Havre. The entrance to the outer harbour, from the jetties and looking towards Deauville, can be seen in *The Port of Trouville, Low Tide, Morning*, 1889 (pl. 64). With the sea behind him Boudin painted this view from Deauville jetty. The river curves round and disappears into the outer harbour to the left and immediately ahead is the lock with the main dock area beyond. To the left is the tall slim tower of the lighthouse while on the right, the large and commanding port building provides a necessary area of stability and a focal point.

One of Boudin's earliest paintings of the port is *The Quay at Trouville*, *c.* 1864–6 (pl. 63). The view here is from the Pointe de la Cahotte, looking up-river along the quayside. The small, square, tent-like structure, which served as the Le Havre steamship office, is in the middle distance with the distinctive fishmarket just behind it. The curving line of the houses along the quayside and the suggestion of the river lead the viewer's eye into the background. Fashionably dressed figures, the merest flickers of paint, return from the market or have just disembarked from the steamer at the quayside. Like his early jetty paintings, this view of the port involved a variety of subjects and perhaps for that

61.
The Port of Trouville
1873
Oil on panel, 32×58cm
The National Gallery of Scotland, Edinburgh

reason Boudin did not return to the topic.

On the other hand, by far the most popular view of the port and one which he did explore in countless variations is that seen in *The Port of Trouville*, 1873 (pl. 61). Here Boudin worked from the bridge over La Touques, from the Deauville side, and looked down-river past the line of quays on the right with the Pointe de la Cahotte forming the background. The long warehouse on the point is easily distinguished as is the Hôtel Bellevue.

One of these variants is *The Port of Trouville, Boatyard*, *c.* 1885–90, painted from a similar position but from a narrower angle (pl. 62). In the late 1860s the boatyard moved from the Pointe de la Cahotte to this site further up-river on the Deauville bank. In the foreground rowing boats add notes of strong colour to the green of the bank. Behind them, on a slipway, a large wooden hull is being built with some tiny figures of people looking on. At the quayside, on the right, the sails of fishing boats march off into the

distance, echoing the line of houses curving round towards the centre of Trouville. The mood is one of calm, a period of rest. Boudin always preferred, where possible, to avoid the noise and bustle of a working port, painting it instead when the dock workers and fishermen had already gone.

62.

The Port of Trouville, Boatyard
*c.*1885–90, Oil on canvas, 40.5×55.5cm
McLean Art Gallery and Museum, Greenock

63.

The Quay at Trouville
*c.*1864–6
Oil on panel, 27×38cm
Galerie Apesteguy, Deauville

64.

The Port of Trouville, Low Tide, Morning
1889
Oil on canvas, 41×55cm
Private Collection

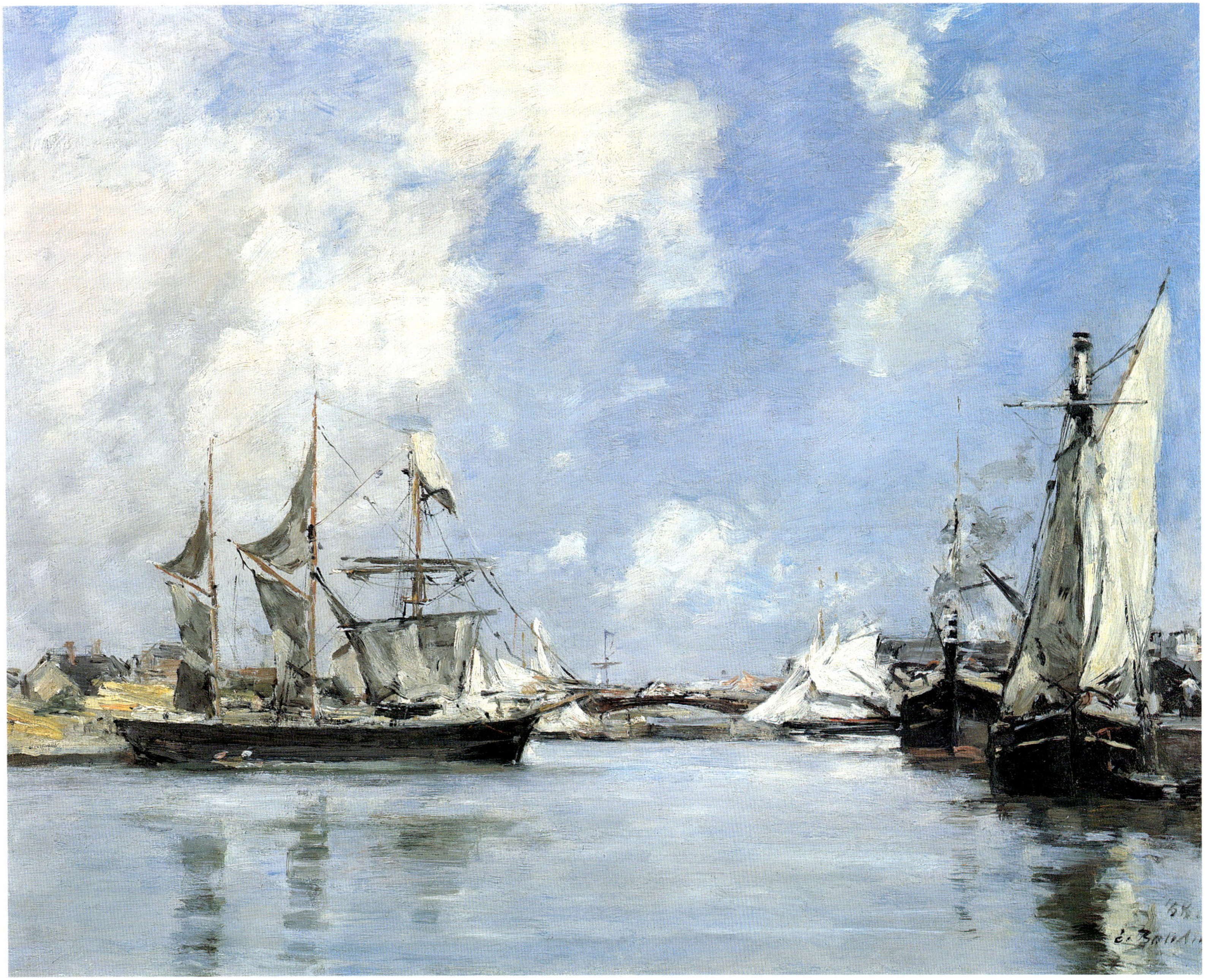

65.
Deauville, The Dock
1888
Oil on panel, 33×41.5cm
Richard Green Gallery, London

66.

Deauville, The Dock
1891
Oil on panel, 27.9×21.9cm
Glasgow Museums: The Burrell Collection

67.

The Lock at Trouville
1894, Oil on panel, 32.5×41.5cm
Galerie Apesteguy, Deauville

# 10. The Fishmarket

*It is only his paintings which are referred to here but his drawings and his slightest sketches must also be looked at; a nothing, a nimbly drawn pen or pencil line; here and there something a little thicker which resembles a spot and there it is; you are looking at the motif, figure, seascape or landscape encountered and portrayed.*

Dalligny[1]

The first decree regulating the sale of fish in Trouville dates from 18 April 1841. The following year, the mayor, Florentin Couyère, decided that a fishmarket should be built on the quay in front of the rue des Bains. A project for a modest wooden market, with slim posts supporting a zinc-covered roof, and with a central campanile carrying a clock and bell, was presented and the structure duly erected (pl. 69).

On 20 November 1844 a decree proclaimed that 'the display and sale of fish, shellfish and sea birds shall not be permitted anywhere except in the fishmarket built for this purpose.'[2] The fishmarket, like the jetty, was of interest to the holidaymakers: 'The reason for talking about this cramped and unimportant little market is certainly not its architecture but its curiosity value for the bathers. The side facing the rue des Bains is occupied by the retailers. The actual market is on the port side. There, from six o'clock in the morning when the fishing boats arrive and the fish is unloaded, the bell is rung to signal the start of the auction, a very curious sight for the observer. One point to note is that the prices asked decrease, contrary to normal practice'. [3]

Boudin, like other visitors to Trouville, was drawn to the fishmarket. In his notebooks he recorded ideas for subjects to pursue, frequently writing notes to himself on the kind of preparation he would first need to undertake. Often inspired by visits to the Louvre or to exhibitions, or by conversations with artist friends, these brief statements disclose much about Boudin's working method and his artistic aims. Several short sentences, written in the 1860s, reveal his interest in the theme of fishmarkets:

'Fishmarkets. Ponder that in different ways, whether having figures predominate or focusing all the attention on the fish. This must be prepared on the spot to have exactly the right people and props.'

68.
The Fishmarket at Trouville
1876
Oil on canvas, 33×41cm
Private Collection. Courtesy of Galerie Schmit, Paris

'A large market with the people shown on their striking side. For that all the material must be gathered on the spot.'

'Fishmarkets. There is a gold mine to be exploited. How many have I sketched? If I apply myself I should produce a certain number with figures of a foot or so. Trouville, and Rotterdam – consider.'

'Figures! Figures! Markets in Trouville itself or elsewhere.'[4]

Boudin insists here on his need to understand, not merely to record. By working directly in front of the subject he hopes to seize characteristic types, poses and gestures. An essential tool in this learning process was his use of drawings, watercolours and oil sketches. That he followed his own advice and tried to use 'real life for everything as often as possible' can be seen in the 6,000 magnificent drawings, watercolours and oil sketches in the collection of the Cabinet des dessins in the Louvre.[5] Remaining in Boudin's studio at his death – works he considered as being solely for his own use and consequently not for sale – these studies show a Boudin free from traditional notions of 'finish', intent only on capturing and conveying the essence of the scene unfolding before him.

Of the many subjects covered by these studies some of the most glorious are those of the fishmarket at Trouville. They include quick pencil sketches which establish the main lines of the composition – the angle of vision, whether close to or distant, the proportion

69.
Charles Mozin
The Fishmarket at Trouville
*c.* 1846
Engraving
Musée de Trouville

70.
The Fishmarket at Trouville
Photograph
Bibliothèque Nationale, Paris

71.
Isidore Deroy (1797–1886)
The Quay at Trouville
*c.*1878
Lithograph
Musée de Trouville

72.
The Fishmarket at Trouville
Photograph
Bibliothèque Nationale, Paris

of sky and space to buildings and figures – and hasty inscriptions recording the dominant colours and their placing (pls. 74 and 79). That it is Trouville market and no other is seen by his inclusion of this fishmarket's distinctive clock and bell-tower and by the façades of the houses curving around the quayside. The broad lines of the pencil sketch are then developed further in a watercolour where figures are suggested in long splashes of colour, and the whole is only saved from abstraction by the recognizable market roof and the stalls, and by the masts and sails of boats at the quayside (pl. 76). In all his watercolours the colour of the paper support is frequently left to play a major role.

Boudin studies his subject from all angles, gradually moving closer. From the milling crowds in front of the stalls, a sea of pale green, pink, mustard, mauve, grey and black, he concentrates on the stalls and stall-holders themselves, with the mass of fish a symphony in pink (pls. 77 and 73). Although individual gestures are not distinguishable from the distance, Boudin's ability to record characteristic movements and situations can be seen in his small watercolours of the quayside next to the market. A few quick lines and some hasty washes of colour are all he needs to sum up the tiredness of the horse resting with its cart, the patient watchfulness of the fishermen, the attentiveness of a woman selecting her purchases, and the characteristic baskets, benches, masts and sails that help locate the scene.

The greater part of Boudin's studies show the exterior of the Trouville market but in a number of watercolours and oil sketches and in a few paintings he quite uncharacteristi-

73·
A Fishstall in Normandy
Watercolour and pencil
Département des Arts Graphiques, Louvre

cally chooses to portray its almost claustrophobic interior. In the large hall-like structure there are few distinctive features and very little light, making the scene difficult to read. Boudin's challenge here is to paint darkness rather than light. Colour and movement alone define the subject, the artist deliberately avoiding anecdotal details of costume or action and rejecting artificial illumination.

Despite the quality and the number of studies Boudin executed of this market, his first and only major painting of the subject is *The Fishmarket at Trouville*, 1876 (pl. 68). He never abandoned the subject completely, returning to it in the last decade of his life, struggling to resolve his compositional problems in a series of oil sketches, some of which are today in the collection at Le Havre.

The particular inspiration behind Boudin's paintings of the fishmarket in Trouville is not known. While he might have been influenced by the work of the Dutch masters in the Louvre or by older contemporaries like Mozin or Isabey, it is possible that the idea came from his own experience. The young Boudin would have known the fishmarket in his home town of Honfleur which, located beside the old dock, he recorded in a pastel of about 1859, left at his death to the Honfleur Museum.

74·
The Fishmarket at Trouville
Pencil, 16.7×22.2cm
Département des Arts Graphiques, Louvre

It was not until the late 1860s that Boudin tackled the subject of markets in oil and, despite the evidence of his notebooks and his notion that here was a 'gold-mine' to exploit, he only ever produced 37 signed oils of which 21 are of fishmarkets. In Brittany in the 1860s he painted the local horse and cattle-markets, which with their buildings and frieze-like crowds relate closely in composition to his scenes of *pardons* and marriages. The buildings provide a backdrop on three sides, setting and containing the scene. He takes the subject up again in Brussels in 1870–1 where the distinctive building of the old fishmarket provided a curving backdrop unlike the fishmarket in Rotterdam where, in 1874–6, he recorded the stalls placed under the trees.

As with all his market scenes, whether in Brittany, Brussels or Rotterdam, Boudin was fascinated by the challenge of depicting a crowd, simultaneously catching it in all its diversity and yet preserving the individuality of certain figures. The further challenge was one of avoiding anecdote and yet capturing characteristic movements, gestures, attitudes and costumes.

In *The Fishmarket at Trouville*, 1876, Boudin uses the curving façade of the quayside

75·
Interior of the Old Fishmarket at Trouville
Watercolour and pencil, 11.7×15.6cm
Département des Arts Graphiques, Louvre

houses and the strong diagonal of the fishmarket itself to create and define the space within which the action will take place – almost like a stage (pl. 68). To the right the quay itself is suggested by the dismembered, abstract views of masts and limp sails of fishing vessels which have already disembarked their cargo. A loaded cart is suggested to the right, while in the background the driver of a horse-driven cart or carriage can be seen lifting his whip.

The immediate foreground is left empty of incident, a necessary breathing space between the artist, the viewer and the crowd. In this instance Boudin does not even include a dog in the foreground, for scale and to focus attention on the action of the picture, as he normally does. The viewer must work to discern what is happening, for against the calm stability of the buildings there is a hive of activity and movement. Women, seen from the front and back, come and go, carrying baskets, leading children. Some have stopped to look, to purchase, others to chat, one is even seated on the kerbside. Two men in the left foreground chat, the figure in blue with his back to us echoed by the blue-

76.
The Old Fishmarket at Trouville
Watercolour and pencil, 11.3×15cm
Département des Arts Graphiques, Louvre

coated figure to the right, which, with the woman again with her back to us in the foreground, all encourage the viewer's eye to move on into the picture space itself.

Boudin is interested in the picturesque buildings and fascinated by the light and by the stormy sky which sets the mood. He enjoys the play of light and shade: the dark figures, their light bonnets, the deep shade under the roof and the last rays of light, before the storm, hitting off the façades of the houses. He contrasts the straight lines of the buildings, the many and varied heights, angles and slopes of the roofs, against the roundness of the human forms. There is also a conscious repetition of the triangular shape of the zinc-covered fishmarket roof and of the canvas roofs of the stalls with the inverted and limp triangles of the sails.

The painting is a remarkably accurate representation of the old fishmarket at Trouville. The original market of 1843 was replaced by a new building in 1881. This structure was further developed in the late 1890s and was in turn replaced by another larger building in 1936. Most of Boudin's Trouville fishmarket scenes, executed between

77.
A Quay at Trouville
Watercolour and pencil, 14.3×18.7cm
Département des Arts Graphiques, Louvre

1868 and 1878, show the old market. It is interesting to note, however, that the few signed oils dating to the mid-1880s still show the old rather than the new market. Rather than assuming that Boudin was deliberately ignoring the changes wrought by time, it is entirely possible that the panels were begun, on the spot, prior to 1881 but were only finished in the studio and signed many years later.

78.

Interior of the Old Fishmarket at Trouville
Watercolour, 13.1×14.4cm
Département des Arts Graphiques, Louvre

79.

The Fishmarket at Trouville
Pencil, 9.5×14.4cm
Département des Arts Graphiques, Louvre

80.

Laundresses by a Stream
*c.*1885–90
Oil on panel, 17.8×22.9cm
The National Gallery, London

# 11. Washerwomen

Although tiny figures of washerwomen can often be glimpsed working at the riverside in the landscapes of artists like Corot and Daubigny, these are rarely, as they are with Boudin, the main subject of the painting. With the exception of a few works painted at Le Faou, Etaples and Etretat, most of Boudin's 130 paintings of the subject show washerwomen on the banks of the river Touques in or near Trouville. There are few drawings or watercolours of these washerwomen, Boudin evidently content to work directly on the canvas without first establishing the broad lines of his composition.

When he first tackled the subject in the 1860s it was as a variant on his studies of the port of Trouville. The women are shown kneeling on the sand near the quayside, at low tide, with beached fishing boats nearby. It was not until 1878 that he embarked on what was to be his most characteristic treatment of the subject. In some 100 paintings he focuses on the women themselves, sometimes as part of a broad panorama as in *Washerwomen on the Banks of the River Touques*, 1884, or in isolation against a bank, as in *Laundresses by a Stream*, *c.*1885–90 (pls. 82 and 80).

In their subject these paintings are the antithesis of Boudin's beach scenes. Unlike the fashionable visitors idling on the sand, these local women are hard at work. Boudin rarely shows them turning to each other and chattering; instead they are seen from behind, their backs bent, intent on their task (pl. 84). Their washing lies beside them in bundles, loaded into a basket, piled high on a stool or spread behind them on fences to dry. With their sleeves rolled up and leaning over the water's edge they rinse their garments in the water, rub them together using the sand as an abrasive or beat them against the stones and rocks. By the nature of their task, these washerwomen provided Boudin with an ideal subject combining as it did observation of the human figure with description of water, sky and landscape. In a series of small, almost repetitive pictures, Boudin explored a variety of colour harmonies, often achieving rich tapestry-like effects.

In a few paintings the washerwomen are seen near a bridge. In *Washerwomen on the Banks of the River Touques*, *c.*1883–7, the artist contrasts the diagonal of the riverbank, which moves back into the picture space and thereby establishes a feeling of depth, with the strong horizontal of the bridge (pl. 81). It is only after a few minutes that the viewer

81.

Washerwomen on the Banks of the River Touques
*c.*1883–7
Oil on panel, 16.5×21.6cm
Glasgow Museums: The Burrell Collection

82.

Washerwomen on the Banks of the River Touques
1884
Oil on panel, 27×40cm
The National Gallery of Scotland, Edinburgh

83.

The Trouville-Deauville Bridge over the River Touques
Photograph
Musée de Trouville

notices how Boudin has subtly suggested a figure who, crossing the bridge, has now stopped to watch the women.

Although the bridge in this painting is similar to that of Touques, the spire glimpsed in the background, the green hill to the right and the beached boats at the quay on the far bank seem to indicate that it is the bridge at Trouville. This first bridge had four arches, one of which could turn to allow ships to move up-river to the port of Touques. Inaugurated in 1863 it was destroyed during the Second World War and was replaced by a concrete bridge.

84.

Washerwomen on the Banks of the River Touques
*c.*1888–95
Oil on panel, 20.6×33cm
Glasgow Museums: The Burrell Collection

# 12. Landscapes

*Eugène Boudin, together with Corot and Jongkind, is one of the immediate precursors of Impressionism. He shows us that impenetrable black does not exist and that air is transparent. He observes the effect of light on objects and how planes are formed as far as the horizon. He portrays the infinite and delightful range of greys, from grey mixed with dark purple to the silver grey of a fish's stomach, and he portrays them successfully; he captures both the movement of objects and their shape and colour: a rising cloud, shimmering water, a dazzling sail in the sunlight, a passing boat and he puts together the elements and beings in action.*

Geffroy[1]

Boudin is rightly recognized as having played a vital role in the history of French landscape painting, in particular in having been one of the first artists to work consistently out of doors from nature. Throughout his career he painted both land and seascapes, though in terms of output, the seascapes far outnumber the landscapes. Not surprisingly, most of Boudin's landscapes include water – rivers, canals or marshes – and extensive skies.

His early views of the Normandy countryside with its thatched cottages and farms show more clearly than any other aspect of his art his debt to the Barbizon artists and to Daubigny and Corot. *The Trouville Road*, *c.*1860–3, in its composition and subject clearly shows the influence of Troyon, with whom Boudin was so closely associated at this period (pl. 85). These various influences continue in his paintings of the rugged coastlines of Brittany and Berck and are still present in the 1890s when he paints the river valleys of Saint-Arnoult and Saint-Valéry-sur-Somme.

Already in the 1870s Boudin had painted views of the river Touques and distant views of the beach and sea from the hill above Trouville. It was here that many new villas were being built for wealthy entrepreneurs like Jacques Cordier. It was a subject Boudin tackled on a number of occasions but none more dramatically than in *The River Touques from Trouville*, 1883 (pl. 87). In the immediate foreground there is an almost abstract play on the angles and planes of the roofs of the houses, half-hidden by trees and by the gradual slope of the hill. Although dissimilar in colour and technique, the composition is reminiscent of some of Cézanne's views of Mont-Saint-Victoire and shows that Boudin could break from traditional compositions when the subject chosen provided the opportunity. There are various paintings too of the roads on this hillside such as *Trouville. The Drovers' Lane*, October 1886, which although reminiscent of early Pissarro is, however, conservative in its composition (pl. 88).

It was only in the later 1880s that Boudin regularly painted the fertile pastures inland from Trouville along the banks of the river Touques. By this time he had firmly established himself as a painter of the beach and port of Trouville and was possibly in search of new challenges. In addition, despite his advancing age and increasing problems with his health, mobility had been made easier. As he himself points out in a letter to his student Braquaval of 12 September 1890, 'I have made several studies of our dead river. There is no shortage of beautiful landscape if you have the courage to go and find it; but for that we have two railway lines, a tram and, if necessary, carriages.'[12]

*The Deauville Road*, 1881 (pl. 86), in composition and tonality is remarkably close to early landscapes by Pissarro. Although Boudin uses the broken brushstroke of the young Impressionists he does not challenge traditional ideas on the role of light or the use of local colour. The composition itself is conservative, the road curving into the distance being a traditional device for establishing depth. Human interest is added in the form of a woman's figure seen from the back, a man at a cottage gate and some figures, one with a dog, coming towards the viewer. Rather than being included for anecdotal interest these figures add a feeling of movement, provide vital notes of colour and establish a sense of scale, the artist's main interest being in depicting the dark grey of the stormy sky against the equally dark greens of the trees.

Throughout his career Boudin, influenced by Troyon, executed large numbers of paintings, and countless studies in oil and pastel, of cows grazing. In much the same way as with the figures on the beach, Boudin was interested in the variety of possible groupings of the animals and was equally fascinated by the rich, warm browns of the cattle against the greens of the landscape. Similar earthy tonalities are employed in *The Water Meadows at Deauville*, *c.*1888–95 where a herd of cows can just be made out lying in the field on the right (pl. 89). The painting sings with rich greens, browns, mustards, terracottas and ochres – the bottom left corner being a veritable autumnal tapestry, one he reverted to regularly in his landscapes.

The sky is pale, almost washed out, its watery blue and its creamy clouds reflected in the river. The paint surface itself is rich and vibrant, with many areas of impasto and a few bristles from Boudin's brush which have adhered to the paint. Boudin's brushstrokes echo the form and create the texture of his subject, wonderfully coarse strokes being used to suggest the reeds beside the small rowing boat. The trees are indicated with a minimum of form in silvery tones of grey and green. Although there are no figures here, a human presence is implied by the boat tied up in the foreground, by the distant buildings and the smoke rising on the horizon.

*The Banks of the River Touques at Trouville*, 1891, like most of the later landscapes, is painted on canvas rather than on panel (pl. 90). The paint surface here is much thinner, the brushstrokes dry and directional. The dominant tones of blue and light, bright green are set off by notes of pink in the path and burgundy in the foreground. Despite its late date Boudin continues to employ a traditional composition, the diagonal of the path set against the strong horizontal of the distant bridge.

85.

The Trouville Road
*c.*1860–3
Oil on canvas, 57×83cm
Musée Eugène Boudin, Honfleur

86.

The Deauville Road
1881, Oil on canvas, 51×61cm
Paisley Museum and Art Gallery

87.
The River Touques from Trouville
1883
Oil on canvas, 55×74.5cm
The Art Institute of Chicago, Gift of F. H. & L. B. Woods

88.
Trouville. The Drovers' Lane
1886,
Oil on canvas, 51×61cm
Private Collection

89.

The Water Meadows at Deauville
*c.*1888–95
Oil on canvas, 50.3×76cm
Graves Art Gallery, Sheffield

90.

The Banks of the River Touques at Trouville
1891
Oil on canvas, 51×74cm
Berwick-upon-Tweed Borough Museum and Art Gallery

91.

Trouville from the Hill
Oil on canvas, 54×74cm
Private Collection

# 13. Fashionable Dress and Boudin

Liz Arthur

Boudin's beach scenes accurately record the fashionable middle and upper classes taking their leisure, promenading and enjoying the sights but also enjoying being seen in the latest fashions. Such paintings are not only a delight in themselves, but are also an invaluable aid to costume historians. With consummate skill Boudin details the fashions of the day and more importantly the lively manner in which they were worn. An understanding of the dress of the period when France dominated fashion and the speed of change was accelerating can enhance our appreciation of Boudin's artistic achievement.

The expansionist years of the 1850s and 1860s and the splendour of the Second Empire are symbolized by that most distinctive of garments, the crinoline. Its exuberance and often outrageous size suited the mood of the times. It was heartily disliked by many men, reviled by the advocates of dress reform and aesthetes of the Pre-Raphaelite movement and lampooned by caricaturists, yet it was probably the first universal fashion worn by women in all walks of life whatever their social status (pl. 92). Despite being impractical and dangerous, it was soon worn by factory workers, shop assistants and household servants.

The cage crinoline is widely associated with the Empress Eugénie who is credited with, or blamed for, encouraging its widespread acceptance. Although she was not a great fashion innovator and the couturier Charles Frederick Worth considered her conservative in her taste, she was the most influential fashionable figure of the day. Of Scottish-Spanish descent and with striking good looks and a sense of style, she gave a new impetus to the French fashion industry. In Boudin's painting thought to be the Empress at Trouville in 1863 we see the crinoline or jupon at its most extravagant (pl. 1).

The underpinnings supporting these ever-widening skirts had developed gradually. Initially several stiffened petticoats (sometimes as many as twelve) were worn. These included the original crinoline which was a petticoat made of horsehair (*crin*). Other devices such as plaited straw, whalebone hoops and inflatable rubber tubes were also tried. However, these were heavy, creaked and rattled, or were inflexible. The most successful support was the cage crinoline made of watchspring steel wire, introduced in

92.

One of 44 prints 'Illustrative of the Crinoline' published by W. H. I. Carter, 12 Regent Street, London
Private Collection

1856. This consisted of graduated horizontal circles of wire held together by vertical bands of tape or ribbon. This construction was lightweight without being cumbersome.

Edward Philpott, Family Draper and Jupon Manufacturer of Piccadilly, advertised his Jewelled Jupon as 'Weighing only 14oz which surely must be a boon to invalids and watering-place belles?' The cage provided the required shape without bulk at the waist and created the illusion of a small waist. To give his products further credibility Philpott claimed that 'The great art critic Mr Ruskin has said that the female dress of the present day [1864] is as near perfection as possible.'[1]

Boudin's paintings capture the swinging rise and fall of the crinoline in motion and he has recorded the outline of the framework where the fabric has been pressed against it by the wind (pl. 101). This is not an artistic invention but is clearly based on first-hand observation.

However, its volume and lightness made the crinoline unpredictable in windy weather and women wearing them were occasionally blown off cliffs or caught in carriage wheels. Yet it was enormously popular and the Saxony branch of Thomson's, the largest crinoline manufacturer, produced over nine and a half million in twelve years. The major benefit of the cage crinoline was that it freed women's legs from the restriction of heavy petticoats and enabled skirts to expand to even greater extremes, much to the delight of *Punch* magazine.

The ease of movement led to new informal styles of dress suited to more active pursuits. The Empress Eugénie, who enjoyed vigorous country and seaside walks, much to the disgust of some of her ladies-in-waiting, is said to have adopted the new English form of walking dress after a visit to England in 1862 (pl. 945). This is unlikely because this style would already have been familiar to her as it had been worn by Princess Pauline von Metternich at Fontainebleau in 1859. Walking dress had shorter skirts with a system of internal cords passed through rings to enable the skirt to be raised. This was worn in the country, at the seaside, or for croquet and archery. The beach scenes of the early 1860s show that the petticoats revealed were often multicoloured, striped or trimmed with contrasting fabrics, or simply of a bold colour.

More dramatically, as Boudin records, the walking dress revealed ankles and feet which had been concealed for the previous twenty years. This encouraged the wearing

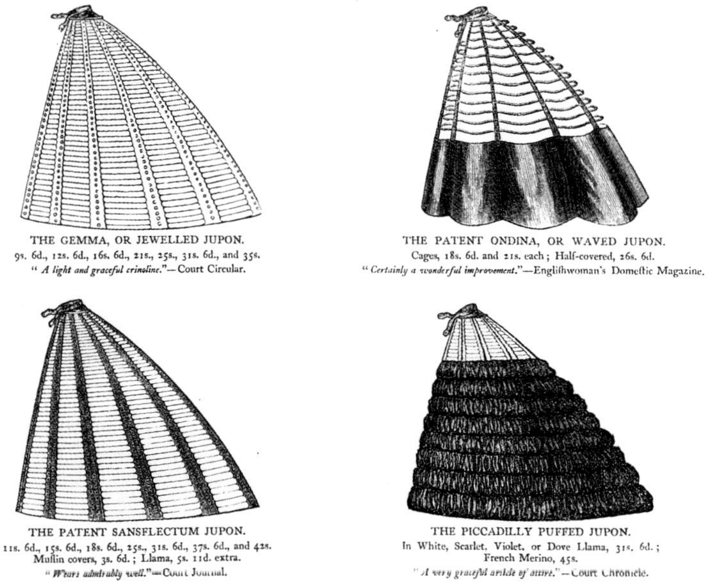


93.
*Crinolines in our Parks & Promenades, from 1710 to 1864*, Edward Philpott, London, 1864
Private Collection

94·
Fashion Plate from the *Englishwoman's Domestic Magazine*, 1865
Private Collection

95·
English walking dress *c.*1857
Photograph, Private Collection

of saucy horizontally striped stockings and brightly coloured, narrow square-toed boots with low heels, in contrast to the simple plain, flat shoes and boots worn since the early nineteenth century (pl. 97). A greater variety of boots became available partly as a result of the growing mechanized production of footwear initiated by Bally at Schoenward in 1851. There were kid leather boots with patent leather toes, or the very fashionable high Polish boots which had coloured heels, were fastened with laces and had tassels at the top. An elastic-sided boot (the forerunner of the Chelsea boot) was worn by both men and women.

Boudin records the bulky reality of seaside or promenade costume, while the graceful ideals were illustrated regularly in the more readily available magazines. Here we see the major creative influence of the period, that of Charles Frederick Worth. He disliked the crinoline and was responsible for changing its shape from a dome to a fan. He did this by

96.
Photograph, sitter unknown, mid-1860s
Private Collection

introducing a skirt with gored panels. These were cut diagonally across the length of the fabric for economy, and concentrated the fullness at the back. He also used the princess style in which bodice and skirt were constructed without a waist seam. He simplified the trimmings and, as shawls, short silk mantles or loose jackets called *paletots* were worn, the decoration was confined to the lower part of the skirt (pl. 94). This usually took the form of simple bold angular patterns in bands of appliquéd ribbon or velvet, or a pleated flounce. He encouraged the change from elaborate, lightweight brocades to plainer, heavier silks such as *moiré antique*.

Worth, whose restrained style contrasted with the elaborate dress previously in vogue at court, was introduced to the Empress Eugénie in 1860 by the Princesse de Metternich, the chic wife of the Austrian ambassador. Once patronized by the Empress Worth's success was assured. He changed the role of the fashion designer from a fairly humble one to that of arbiter of fashion. The son of an impecunious Lincolnshire solicitor, Worth opened a fashion house in rue de la Paix, Paris, and established *haute couture*.

Large numbers of official functions and receptions provided the opportunity for extravagant display and Empress Eugénie is known to have encouraged visitors never to be seen in the same dress twice, which meant four changes each day. Although most good quality silk dresses usually had two bodices, one for day, the other for evening, this still meant enormous expense. In effect the luxurious excesses of the court enhanced its prestige, supported the textile manufacturers and encouraged the fashion industry. This, together with the creative influence of Worth and new technical developments, ensured the supremacy of French fashion throughout the Western world.

The introduction of the improved sewing machine and paper patterns allowed the working and lower middle classes to aspire to the styles in Boudin's beach scenes. Most women's clothes were still made by local dressmakers although mass production methods were being introduced. However, these methods were still in their infancy and their use was confined to the production of mantles, jackets, men's and children's clothing and mourning wear, all of which were available in the new large department stores. Many mistresses complained of pretentious servants and that it was impossible to distinguish between themselves and their off-duty maids (pl. 99). While many of the fashionable clothes exist few working garments survive.

However, Boudin also recorded the dress of fisherfolk and washerwomen. On Trouville beach he saw many nannies with their charges and included them in his paintings (pl. 41). They are easily distinguished by their white caps tied under the chin, plain, unadorned dark dresses and long white aprons. In the later paintings we can see how

97.
Fashion Plate from *Le Follet*, *c.*1866
Private Collection

98.
Fashion Plate from the *Journal des Tailleurs*, July 1860
Private Collection

these have been formalized into a uniform. On the left of the *Figures beside the Marquee at Trouville Casino* (Musée Eugène Boudin, Honfleur), 1884, the nurse now wears a cap with ribbons, a simple cotton dress with a white collar and an apron with a bib and shoulderstraps.

It is impossible to distinguish between small boys and girls in Boudin's paintings as they traditionally wore identical dresses until the age of about four or five. This was presumably for practical reasons in the days before plastic pants. After this boys wore tunics and trousers while, as we see from the mother and daughter in the centre of *Approaching Storm*,1864, girls were dressed like miniature adults, even while playing on the beach (pl. 32).

Although these clothes appear over-elaborate and unsuitable to our eyes, there were a

"LIKE HER IMPUDENCE."

*Missis and the Young Ladies (together).* "GOODNESS GRACIOUS, J'MIMA! WHAT HAVE YOU——*WHERE'S* YOUR CR'N'LIN!" (*This word snappishly.*)
*Jemima.* "OH 'M, PLEASE 'M, WHICH I UNDERSTOOD AS THEY WAS A GOIN' OUT, 'M——" [*Receives warning on the spot.*

HOW WOULD IT BE WITHOUT CRINOLINE?—TRY IT FOR 1864!

99.
*Punch*, 14 July 1866
Private Collection

100.
*Punch's Almanack for 1864*
Private Collection

few practical concessions to the conditions and the informal occasion. In general people had far fewer clothes and took greater care of them. Clothes were regularly brushed and sponged and women's everyday wear had woollen brush braid stitched around the hem to protect it. This braid had to be replaced when worn, a tedious task as skirts were often as much as five yards in circumference. For children and adults white piqué cotton or cotton duck was popular because it stood up to the sand and sea and washed easily.

Men's fashions were slower to change than women's, but they too were affected by the need for less formal styles and fabrics. Short, square-cut lounge jackets with high, narrow lapels, reefer or pea jackets, Norfolk and tweed suits, were all new introductions, but all were worn with starched collars and ties (pl. 98). The older men can be seen still in their formal frock coats and top hats while the younger men have adopted the innovations. The writer for an English magazine observed the men on Trouville beach in 1874: 'People of all nations saunter along the boarded walk across the sand – Frenchmen in light blue suits, white boots and small thermometers fastened to their hat bands; Englishmen in "loud" patterns; Russians in top boots, red sashes, and white duck jackets . . .'[2]

Everyone on the beach, including the children, wears a hat. Many of the men wear low-crowned bowlers introduced in the 1850s and named after T. & W. Bowler of Southwark, London, the feltmakers who made the originals. The bowler was introduced as an intermediate style between the formal top hat and the very informal wideawake hat. Some of the men wear straw hats, but the women enjoyed greater choice.

Neat spoon-shaped bonnets which had enclosed the head and neck and formed the apex of the all-enveloping triangular silhouette throughout the 1850s gave way to the hat. It may seem extraordinary at a time when women revealed expanses of bare shoulder in the evening that it was considered quite a dramatic change to reveal the nape of the neck out of doors, but for many years bonnets had acted as a frame for the face and sported a frill (*bavolet*) to conceal the back of the neck. Fanchon bonnets, made without *bavolets*, were said to have been introduced by Worth and first worn by his wife. These allowed the hair to be drawn back from the face *à l'impératrice* and dressed in a chignon, appropriately caught in a net, often of chenille, decorated with pearls or shells. This was a style which boosted the sale of false hair pieces.

The most popular form of hat was the pork-pie shape, of silk, plush or velvet, constructed on a straw foundation and trimmed with a feather. It can be seen in all of the 1860s scenes. Hats were tilted forward at a jaunty angle, often tied on under the chignon with narrow ribbons. There were also the broad-brimmed forms such as the Leghorn Gypsy hat, or 'seaside hat', of crinoline cloth or Leghorn straw with a cord at the front which could be held in windy weather. These flat, wide-brimmed hats are of rustic origin, derived either from the *bergère* eighteenth-century shepherdess, or inspired by the traditional peasants' hat from the south of France and known as the Niçoise. Such hats were therefore always considered more appropriate to informal occasions. Among the most popular trimmings on these coquettish hats were the long ribbons at the back known as 'Follow me lads' which are seen fluttering in so many of the beach scenes.

Another form of seaside headgear seen at the extreme right of *Approaching Storm*, 1864, is the capeline, a light hood with attached cape usually of brightly coloured cashmere or barège trimmed with either ruched ribbon or braid. But none of these protected the complexion and so parasols and veils were used. Occasionally separate stiffened silk brims known as uglies were worn with bonnets, but these seem to have been more popular with the British.

Although the fashion industry was not directly affected by the European wars, several of the new women's garments were inspired by military figures or borrowed from men's wear. There was the Zouave, or Spanish jacket, similar to a bolero, derived from the Algerian volunteer regiment which fought for the French in the Crimea, and the Burnous mantle trimmed with tassels. The red Garibaldi blouse and pill-box cap (known as a *casquette*) became fashionable for informal wear in 1860 after the invasion of Sicily by the Italian nationalist hero, and Hussar braid trimming was frequently used throughout the 1860s. All were considered suitable for country or seaside wear and all are documented in Boudin's work.

The intensity of the newly invented aniline dyes is captured by Boudin in vivid accents of colour. These dyes were extremely popular because they made available shades which were difficult to achieve with vegetable or mineral dyes. They were often given newsworthy names such as Sebastopol blue, or Solferino and Magenta, named after Napoleon III's victories over the Austrians in 1859. In France it was considered inappropriate to have more than two colours in one outfit but the British often wore many more and were condemned by the French for their lack of taste.

On the other hand the British criticized the French bathers at Trouville: 'From the canvas bathing-house there issue at high water the ladies in "bloomer" costumes and straw hats, who are careful to let neither their faces nor their hair touch the salt water, who swim with one foot on the bottom, and who never bathe without an escort of male friends.'[3]

The new Zouave Marine swimming costume superseded the earlier traditional long blue bathing dress which often clung to the body or rode up in the waves. It consisted of 'a body and trousers cut in one, which secures perfect liberty of action and does not expose the figure'.[4] There were several variations, but most had short sleeves, a belt and either a basque or a short overskirt. They were usually of serge or flannel trimmed with worsted braid. Boudin includes few bathers in his paintings but three typical examples can be seen in *The Bathing Hour, Trouville*, 1864 (pl. 37).

By the mid-1860s a peplum or overskirt was introduced. It was worn over a matching petticoat with a train which gave further emphasis to the back of the dress. There were efforts at court to revive classical styles reminiscent of the First Empire, but these did not catch on. The crinoline had reached its zenith and within a short time it was abandoned altogether (pl. 100). However, it was quickly discovered that skirts did not hang gracefully without support and the fullness was caught up and draped over a crinolette or tornure which eventually became the bustle. This new vertical line is worn by the group of women standing at the right of *The Beach at Trouville* (Private Collection), 1869. By comparing this work with those of four or five years earlier it is possible to chart the process of change, and the accuracy of Boudin's observations becomes obvious. Even in his paintings from the 1880s when his handling is much freer he nevertheless captures the essence of the style. It is still possible to gain an accurate impression of the vertical line, the texture created by frills and trimmings and the tight fit of the garments which were now being worn over longer, more rigid corsets.

Boudin's interest in capturing the feeling of the clothes worn gives particular vitality to the fashionable scenes which he so obviously enjoyed and which he painted.

101.

The Jetty at Trouville
1865
Watercolour and pencil, 15.5×26.5cm
Private Collection

# 14. Boudin's Watercolours of Beaches

Laurent Manoeuvre

The beach scene as treated by Boudin was a new, distinctive and unprecedented subject, as transient in the history of painting as Watteau's *fête galante*. The comparison is not without significance. Boudin made a copy of Watteau's *Embarkation for the Island of Cythera* (Louvre, Paris), which he kept all his life and bequeathed to the museum in his home town. In addition to a matchless skill in painting and drawing, both artists were attracted to the elegance of fragile and transient images: tall female figures dressed in fine fabrics which were to be mercilessly swept aside by fashion; fading dusks; bursts of sun which clouds are about to obscure. There is a temptation to qualify their vision of a world of simple pleasures as superficial; their subtle poetry is only revealed by taking a longer look. Nothing happens in these works; time stands still. Conversations are carried away on the wind, music is lost in the evening air. Movements are frozen as if by a camera lens. A second later everything would have changed while nothing would have really been different: a closed parasol, an empty chair, a figure turned the other way, someone else standing up.

The sudden appearance of the subject of beaches, as if by magic, is an enigma. For years art historians have tried to find the sources of this phenomenon – the names mentioned most often are those of Isabey and Jongkind.

The Dutch tradition of depicting beaches goes back to the Golden Age – the seventeenth century – but is almost exclusively concerned with the world of fishermen. Because of his nationality Jongkind was naturally familiar with these works but, unlike Boudin, had little if any interest in them. Boudin's passion for the Dutch masters possibly began when collectors from Le Havre commissioned copies of Dutch paintings from him with which to decorate their homes. Boudin's accounts show that at the start of his career he was able to make a living from these copies. He later made watercolour copies of Dutch paintings which he discovered during his travels.[1] The Dutch model was to be one of the foundations of Boudin's art, something he never questioned. Surprisingly, from his study of and respect for the Old Masters, Boudin was to acquire a definite taste for the contemporary, and he justified this penchant for modernity by using their example. In 1868, for instance, when talking about his beaches which at the time were causing much debate among certain critics and collectors, he wrote: 'This endeavour is not new because the Italians and the Flemish did nothing but paint their contemporaries.'[2]

Isabey, to the great delight of his contemporaries, practised pastiche brilliantly. Never has 'in the style of' been as popular as during the Second Empire, as if reality were becoming too bitter to be worth depicting directly. Besides his numerous references to sources from the past, Isabey's *Noblemen on the Beach at Scheveningen* (Louvre, Paris) is interesting on more than one count. First of all, there is its date – 1860 – the very year in which Boudin drew his first beach scene. Second, there is the pile of fish in the foreground, something which appeared subsequently in Boudin's work. Third, there are the little dogs chasing each other on the shore. They too appear in Boudin's work with few modifications. For the rest, Isabey lapses into the anecdotal (the nobleman discussing the purchase of fish) and the theatrical (dress and the arrangement of the boats), things with which Boudin was little concerned. In 1868 Boudin even expressed anger at Isabey's obsession for 'searching out gaudy carnival clothes'.[3]

There is another possible source for the beach scene which is never mentioned because the person in question remained almost outside the history of art. In a letter to Boudin, his friend Ferdinand Martin claimed not exactly to have invented the subject but to have provided encouragement to continue along these lines: 'I was the first to urge you to draw beaches.'[4] Apparently in his reply Boudin did not deny this claim, possibly to avoid spoiling a great friendship. This friendship was sometimes hard to understand, in particular when it came to judging the degree of finish and perfection of a work of art. Boudin entrusted Martin, a man of independent means, with the management of his income.[5] Perhaps he also decided to trust his friend's practical and business sense in the field of art. Martin was not only a financier; he was one of the principal members of the Société des amis des arts du Havre, a society which despite its distance from Paris showed singular judgement in 1868 when it exhibited Manet's *The Dead Man* (National Gallery of Art, Washington), several of Monet's works and eight of Courbet's canvases. What is remarkable is that Manet was awarded a silver medal and Monet a bronze, awards which these two masters were not accustomed to receiving.

It is interesting that the first known beach scene by Boudin is a pastel, dated 1860.[6] Taking the beach as a subject represented an important stylistic break, for until this time Boudin's robust and heavy figures – Norman fishermen or Breton farmers – came directly from the world of Millet. The thick, round and confused lines emphasize the denseness of a universe marked by the play of light and dark. At that time Boudin depicted light in relation to shadow, and the latter often predominated. This style of drawing coincided with some of the most depressing years of Boudin's life, years of both mental and financial hardship.

When he ventured into the world of colour he used pastel, a thick and strong material, almost exclusively. To quote Baudelaire, '[these are] pictures of beautiful weather, a perfectly objective and calm vision, so many chaotic darknesses, gaping furnaces, and horizons in mourning'. The poet no doubt found in these pastels an affinity with his own state of mind. For Boudin this recognition and understanding must have acted as a powerful driving force which helped him to emerge from his long period of doubt and hesitation.

Shortly after 1860 his drawing becomes sharp and incisive. The fragmented contours let in the vivid shore light, dissolving forms – ethereally extended silhouettes of elegant city-dwellers. This style became more marked after 1863 when Boudin turned to watercolour. A medium new to him, watercolour was perfectly suited to his subject, the transparency of the medium enhancing the impression of light. Boudin moved out from the shadows to concentrate his attentions on reflections: fine, brightly coloured fabrics on sand flooded with sun, and the sky on the sea. Everything became light. Impressionism was on its way.

At first it is only in the beach scenes that Boudin's development can be seen. During the same period he drew interiors of Breton houses influenced by Rembrandt: semi-darkness predominates, broken here and there by a few patches of light – embers in the hearth, women's headwear, open windows or doors. For these subjects the artist used coloured paper and a palette with predominantly dark colours. The work produced by Boudin in Brittany seems dated in comparison with his work in Normandy.

Questions should be asked about the technical developments which are specific to the beaches. As Boudin was not interested in the Romantics, who frequently used watercolour, he knew little if anything about this technique. He was not to discover the works of English artists until four years before his death: 'at the present time there is only one very unusual exhibition of the English School. Turner, Constable and others. I have benefited a great deal from seeing this . . . it is very instructive and we can learn a lot from it.'[7] Jongkind, however, provides an interesting lead. As we have seen, Boudin met him in Honfleur and in Trouville in the autumn of 1862. At this time Jongkind had been painting watercolours for some time, even making his living from it. Perhaps he persuaded

Boudin to take up this kind of lucrative work, which would explain the famous quotation: 'Jongkind was beginning to make palatable a type of painting whose rather hard peel hid an excellent and very tasty fruit. I took the opportunity to enter through the door which he had forced open and I began, albeit timidly, to proffer my seascapes.'[8] We should not be misled by the term 'painting' (normally understood to mean oil painting); in his letters Boudin often used this word when referring to watercolours.

There is little doubt that Jongkind's influence stopped there. The cold light which clearly defines form in the Dutch painter's work is far removed from that of Boudin. Jongkind could keep his works with vanishing perspectives; Boudin preferred pictures made of superimposed layers, a technique learnt from Corot. Here, only the degree of precision of form creates the illusion of depth.

Etching was another possible influence in the development of Boudin's approach to drawing. Even though only one etching is extant, undated, Boudin's letters prove that he did try this technique in 1864 at the request of Cadart.[9] Here again, Jongkind may have played a role. On 3 December 1862 Jongkind wrote to Boudin: 'Thank you for your compliments on my etchings.'[10] The relative discipline involved in working on copper may have led Boudin to make his lines finer and more focused.

The interest of French art collectors in watercolours proves that the clientele was changing. Admittedly, many of those who bought these works had not inconsiderable incomes, though not sufficient to enable them to collect oil paintings. As befitted their incomes they lived in apartments of relatively modest proportions better suited to the smaller format of the watercolour. Given these circumstances, Boudin could have made watercolour replicas of his ambitious pictures. Instead he treated each watercolour of the beach as a work in its own right, regardless of the degree of finish. And it was the degree of finish which left something to be desired as far as Boudin's contemporaries were concerned. In 1868, quite late in his beach period, Boudin announced that he was going to 'Harpignies, a skilled watercolourist who must give me some good tips'.[11] His method of painting was too free for the collectors, who preferred to decorate their houses with oil painting substitutes. 'If my colour drawings were real watercolours I would already have made a thousand francs this year, maybe more because I was offered a very good price for finished work of this kind.'[12]

Although there are numerous Boudin watercolours of beach scenes in public and private collections, there were few amongst the more than 6,000 drawings left in his studio at his death. Bequeathed by Boudin to the Louvre, these watercolours of beaches are generally considered to be studies for paintings. In reality that is not the case at all.

Unlike the other drawings which Boudin used in his studio, all or nearly all bear a date, indicating that Boudin hoped to sell them – collectors wanted signed and dated works. In fact these watercolours had been left unsold.

They give some indication of the restricted taste of most of the collectors in the last century. Contemporary works and familiarity with Far Eastern art have accustomed us to rather free artistic interpretations. But we need to put ourselves in the shoes of people living at a time when Emperor Napoleon III expressed enthusiasm for products of industrial art from which all trace of human influence had been erased. Many artists tried to compete with machines, even if these were cameras. Technical prowess became outrageously ostentatious, while painters like Manet asserted their creative identity, seeking in this way to differentiate themselves from the craftsmen. It was no longer a question of smooth brushstrokes; an apparent and often calculated haste became compulsory. Boudin worked in his studio but tried hard not to 'alter the touch and the vitality' of the sketch.[13] He was to reject contour, a legacy of ancient sculpture, beloved by the academicians and also by Courbet (unlike Manet): 'Splash on the colour, use fewer contours! . . . Apply the colour in all its glory, in generous proportions.'[14]

Another aim of contemporary artists, which seems to contradict the first one, was faithfulness to colour and to the permutations of light. To achieve this they often worked from life: 'three brushstrokes from life are worth more than two days' work at the easel'.[15] Boudin's words have been quite widely quoted, perhaps too widely. Even though he hated finishing, the artist worked a lot in his Paris studio. It was then that the drawings played an important role because Boudin considered 'as direct paintings things done on the spot or based on a very recent impression'.[16] He drew much from life, probably to be better able to soak up the atmosphere of the place. Although notes on colours, remarks on the light and even the artist's impressions were included, the drawings were rarely directly related to paintings. They were there to create and recreate the atmosphere. Boudin also sketched on canvas from life. Later, in the calm of his studio, he went over everything, glanced through his notes and finished the painting.

It is possible that some watercolours of beaches had a similar purpose, groups drawn in watercolour repeated, though slightly altered in paintings or vice versa. At first glance there seem to be few if any cases of this, but, it must be said, this has not yet been studied systematically.

However, it is worth noting that most of the watercolours of beaches, including those not kept in the studio and even some of the most finished ones, have notes on colours. This indicates that Boudin did not paint in watercolour from life, or at least not completely. His handwriting blends in particularly well with the style of his drawings, and the notes are unobtrusive. Collectors accepted works on which the artist had deliberately left colour indications which he could quite easily have erased before applying watercolour.

We should not forget that, for a time, Boudin sold paper and supplies to artists: 'You can paint watercolours on any kind of paper at all . . . if you want blocks, you have the paper cut to the right size at the shop, then you have three sides gummed and you are ready to begin.'[17] Indeed, a certain number of watercolours were painted on pieces of magazine covers salvaged by the artist. Boudin had the same problem as far as colours were concerned: 'There are very small English paintboxes with square compartments for each colour. This is all very well but they do not last: I have gone back to the French colour blocks which last longer.'[18]

For seven years – not a long time in a career which extended over half a century – Boudin offered his drawings of beaches for sale. This established his reputation despite the fact that he did a considerable amount of other work to make a living. 'I shall do other things but I shall always be the painter of beaches.'[19] He remained for many the painter of beaches, sometimes too exclusively. In fact, after 1870 Boudin progressively abandoned his beaches populated by city-dwellers to concentrate on fishermen and ports. After the beach interlude he simply returned to subjects which had been dear to him for a long time.

Amongst his very first drawings, almost certainly before 1846, there had already been work inspired by the life of the fishermen in Sainte-Adresse. Given Boudin's background such an interest is not surprising. Although the Normandy countryside merges with the shoreline, there is no such merging of thought processes. The rural community whose narrow-mindedness was cruelly described by Flaubert and by Maupassant remained forbidden territory to those who were not part of it. Boudin was no exception to this rule. All he saw of the life of the farmers was when they brought their harvested produce and livestock to town on fair and market days. Boudin wanted to paint what he knew. He saw fishermen every day and knew their fears, their problems and the dangers which they faced. However, he showed them sitting on the jetty or leaning against their boats, chatting as if without a care in the world. It is worth noting that for this man whose life for a long time bordered on the destitute, painting was always a celebration. He wrote to his pupil and friend Braquaval: 'Impressions of winter may be attractive to a dreamer but it is not necessary to put them on canvas. People want to be cheered up and amused in our world – sad people have no place there.'[20] From the hard life of Breton farmers, he depicted the *pardons* where the multicoloured costumes stood out against the granite of the churches.

Between 1854 and 1859 he visited Honfleur and the surrounding area – Sainte-Adresse and sometimes Etretat – amassing his studies of fishermen without a clearly defined aim other perhaps than to create an ambitious painting for the Salon. But this enormous mass of drawings produced few paintings, and in these the sky was more important than the fishermen.

From then on Boudin wanted to paint and draw abstract things – the play of reflections and colours reduced to a whole scale of greys. The man who called himself, with some justification, the painter of grey, turned his back on the bright colours which were inevitably prominent in scenes of beaches populated by city-dwellers. At the same time his approach to drawing became more serious, supplies of paper more important. After 1880 Boudin was only to make use of the white and silver-grey of the lead mine in his drawings. When he saw shrimp fishermen on the beach he reduced them to a flickering of shapes which were little more than abstract marks. At the same time, between 1881 and 1888, when he drew and painted herds of cattle in fields warmed by the sun, he used the same phenomenon, the light reduced to mere coloured spots. At the end of the 1880s Monet and Pissarro came to the same conclusions. Pissarro took a harder line, developing towards Neo-Impressionism. Monet developed a dreamlike world increasingly detached from reality. Boudin limited his discovery to his private work, oil sketches and drawings. When Kandinsky crossed the decisive line into Abstraction in 1911 it was with a watercolour.

# Notes

## 1. BOUDIN: AN INTRODUCTION

1. Boudin notebook entry for 12 December 1854, quoted in G. Jean-Aubry, *Eugène Boudin d'après des documents inédits: l'homme et l'oeuvre*, Paris, 1968, p.21.
2. Gustave Cahen, *Eugène Boudin: sa vie et son oeuvre*, Paris, 1900, p.194.
3. Cahen, p.128.
4. Boudin, autobiographical notes, quoted in Paul Leroi, 'Salon de 1887', *L'Art*, Vol. 43, 1887.
5. From a transcript of a letter to Braquaval of 30 June 1894, private collection.
6. Letter to F. Martin of 29 December 1885, quoted in Jean-Aubry, 1968, p.107.
7. Letter to F. Martin of 15 December 1864, quoted in Jean-Aubry, 1968, p.54.
8. Letter to L. Boudin of 20 April 1868, quoted in Jean-Aubry, 1968, p.65.
9. Letter to F. Martin of 21 November 1879, quoted in Jean-Aubry, 1968, p.94.
10. Letter to F. Martin of 7 February 1883, quoted in Jean-Aubry, 1968, p.100.
11. Cahen, p.122.
12. Letter to L. Boudin of 27 April 1893, quoted in Laurent Manoeuvre, *Eugène Boudin, dessins*, Paris, 1992, p.208.
13. From a transcript of a letter to Braquaval of 16 June 1896, private collection.
14. From a transcript of a letter to Braquaval of 25 October 1889, private collection.
15. From a transcript of a letter to Braquaval of 24 April 1898, private collection.
16. Letter to Louveau from Beaulieu-sur-Mer, 15 May 1898, in Jean-Aubry transcript notes, private collection.
17. Copy of Felix Buhot article in *Journal des Arts*, 14 July 1900, in Salle de documentation, Musée d'Orsay.

## 2. BOUDIN'S MODERNITY

1. Baudelaire, 'Salon de 1859', reprinted in *Ecrits sur l'art*, Paris, 1971, II, pp.93–5.
2. Cahen, pp.181 and 183.
3. Letters and notes made for Braquaval, 1888–96, quoted in Gilbert de Knyff, *Eugène Boudin raconté par lui-même: sa vie, son atelier, son oeuvre*, Paris, 1976, pp.345–54.
4. Cahen, pp.191, 193 and 185.
5. Boudin, autobiographical notes, quoted in Paul Leroi, 'Salon de 1887', *L'Art*, Vol. 43, 1887, p.31.
6. Letter to F. Martin of 11 September 1888, quoted in G. Jean-Aubry, *Eugène Boudin d'après des documents inédits: l'homme et l'oeuvre*, Paris, 1922, p.96.
7. Cahen, p.185
8. Jean-Aubry, 1922, p.35.
9. Jean-Aubry, 1922, p.57.
10. Baudelaire, p.95.
11. Baudelaire, 'Le Peintre de la vie moderne', especially section III, 'L'Artiste, homme du monde, homme des foules et enfant', in *Ecrits sur l'art*, Paris, 1971, II, pp.139–49.
12. A. Schanne, *Souvenirs de Schaunard*, Paris, 1886, pp.231–2.
13. Letter to F. Martin of 3 September 1868, quoted in Jean-Aubry, 1922, p.70.
14. Letter to F. Martin of 25 August 1867, quoted in Jean-Aubry, 1922, p.65. Boudin's diary from this visit to Brittany is published as 'A propos du centenaire de Boudin: Notes d'un voyage en Bretagne (1867)', *Mercure de France*, 15 July 1924, pp.325–53; see also Denise Delouche, *Eugène Boudin et la Bretagne*, URSA, 1987.
15. For a brief discussion of coastal commerce, see Daniel Finamore, 'Maritime Normandy', in Peter C. Sutton, *Boudin: Impressionist Marine Paintings*, exhibition catalogue, Peabody Museum, Salem, Mass., 1991, pp.11–13.
16. See letters to F. Martin of 20 February 1861 and 17 February 1865, quoted in Jean-Aubry, 1922, pp. 49 and 61.
17. Gautier, 'La Rue Laffitte', *L'Artiste*, 3 January 1858, p.10.
18. Letter from Bonvin to Martinet of 22 April 1861, in Etienne Moreau-Nelaton, *Bonvin raconté par lui-même*, Paris, 1927, p.58.
19. See letters to F. Martin of 20 February 1861, to his brother, 3 May 1861, 25 March 1865, to F. Martin, 25 April 1869, 16 December 1869, quoted in Jean-Aubry, 1922, pp. 48–9, 51, 60, 72 and 75. For Boudin's own year-by-year lists of the dealers to whom he was selling, see de Knyff, pp.110–15 (for 1867–71) and pp. 143–7 (for 1872–80).
20. See letter to F. Martin of 10 December 1881, quoted in Jean-Aubry, 1922, p.87; some of Boudin's letters to Durand-Ruel are published in Lionello Venturi, *Les Archives de l'impressionnisme*, Paris, 1939, II, pp.77–92.
21. Letter from Duret to Pissarro of 15 February 1874, quoted in John Rewald, *The History of Impressionism*, New York and London, 1973, p.310.
22. Letter to F. Martin of 26 March 1868, quoted in Jean-Aubry, 1922, p.66; on the Caen sale, see Boudin's witty account to Martin of 26 June 1862, quoted in Jean-Aubry, 1922, pp.53–4; Boudin's auction sales are listed in de Knyff, p.379.
23. See John House, 'Impressionism and its Contexts', in *The Courtauld Collection*, New Haven and London, 1987, p.16.
24. Letter to F. Martin of 20 February 1861, quoted in Jean-Aubry, 1922, p.48.
25. For this distinction in Monet's work, see John House, *Monet:Nature into Art*, London and New Haven, 1986, pp.159–66.

## 3. NORMANDY AND ITS ARTISTS

1. Letter to L. Boudin of 5 April 1847; extract of letter in Salle de documentation, Musée d'Orsay, Paris.
2. Letter to L. Boudin of 26 July 1851, from Jean-Aubry transcript notes, quoted in exhibition catalogue, *Eugène Boudin*, Musée Eugène Boudin, Honfleur, 1992, pp. 15–16.
3. Cahen, p.192.
4. Quoted in exhibition catalogue, *Avant l'Impressionnisme, Le préimpressionnisme à Honfleur, 1820–70*, Musée Eugène Boudin, Honfleur, 1991, p.45.
5. Letter to Braquaval of 30 June 1894, quoted in

Manoeuvre, 1992, p.209.
6. Quoted in exhibition catalogue, Patrick Noon, *Richard Parkes Bonington, 'On the Pleasure of Painting'*, Yale Center for British Art, New Haven, 1991, p.116.
7. Ibid.
8. *Avant l'Impressionnisme*, p.73.
9. Quoted in René Paul Huet, *Paul Huet (1803–69), D'Après ses notes, sa correspondance, ses contemporains*, Paris, 1911, p.104.
10. Henri Hamel, 'Le Canton de Trouville-sur-mer vu par des artistes', *Athena*, No. 73, September 1982, p.24.
11. Letter to de Pierrefitte of 25 October 1896, quoted in Jean-Aubry, 1968, p.32.
12. Letter to F. Martin of 3 September 1868, quoted in Jean-Aubry, 1968, p.72.
13. Ibid.
14. Hamel, pp.17–19.
15. *Avant l'Impressionnisme*, p.133.
16. Letter of Mozin, quoted in exhibition catalogue, *Charles Mozin*, Musées de Trouville and Honfleur, 1988, p.81.
17. Ibid.
18. Letter to F. Martin of 26 February 1875, quoted in Jean-Aubry, 1968, p.90.
19. *Avant l'Impressionnisme*, p.52.
20. Letter from Monet to Boudin of 19 May 1859, quoted in Jean-Aubry, 1968, p.28.
21. Letter to de Pierrefitte of 25 October 1896, quoted in Cahen, p.64.
22. Letter to Ribot of 5 June 1890, quoted in Cahen, p.115.
23. Letter to a friend of 12 January 1878, quoted in Jean-Aubry, 1968, pp. 28–30.
24. Cahen, p.28.
25. Boudin entry in notebook for 16 June 1859, quoted in Jean-Aubry, 1968, p.30.
26. Ibid.
27. Quoted in Manoeuvre, p.188.
28. Quoted in Manoeuvre, p.206.
29. Cahen, p.31.
30. Quoted in exhibition catalogue, *Gustave Courbet*, London, 1978, p.40.
31. Paul Mantz, *Gazette des Beaux-Arts*, September 1878.
32. Quoted from a letter published in *Les Amis de Gustave Courbet, Bulletin*, No. 23, Paris-Ornans, 1959.
33. Cahen, pp.61–2.
34. Louis de Fourcaud in *Le Gaulois*, 10 February 1883.
35. Quoted in Manoeuvre, p.199.
36. *Avant l'Impressionnisme*, p.119; and Cahen, pp.43–4.
37. Article by Zola in *La Cloche*, 1872.
38. Cahen, p.41.
39. *Avant l'Impressionnisme*, p.121; and letter to Alfred Stevens of February 1891, quoted in Jean-Aubry, 1968, p.156.
40. Letter from Jongkind to Boudin of 6 June 1863, quoted in Victorine Hefting, *Jongkind, D'Après sa correspondance*, Utrecht, 1969, p.135.
41. Letter from Jongkind to Boudin of 3 December 1862, quoted in Hefting, p.134.
42. Letter from Monet to Boudin of 20 February 1860, quoted in Jean-Aubry, 1968, p.35.
43. Letter from Jongkind to Martin of September 1863, quoted in Hefting, p.141.
44. *Avant l'Impressionnisme*, p.60.
45. Letter from Monet to Geffroy of 8 May 1920; letter in sale at Hôtel Drouot, Paris, 11 June 1982. Excerpt from letter in Salle de documentation, Musée d'Orsay.
46. Letter from Monet to Jean-Aubry, quoted in exhibition catalogue, *Eugène Boudin*, Marlborough Fine Art, London, 1958, p.11.
47. Letter to Braquaval of 10 May 1895, transcript of letter, private collection.
48. Cahen, p.26; Jean-Aubry, 1968, p.35.
49. Letter to F. Martin of 4 May 1868, quoted in Jean-Aubry, 1968, p.66.
50. Letter to F. Martin of 2 January 1872, quoted in Jean-Aubry, 1968, p.82.
51. Letter to F. Martin of 19 June 1886, quoted in Jean-Aubry, 1968, p.107.
52. Letter from Monet to Boudin of 22 August 1892, quoted in Cahen, p.125.
53. Letter from Boudin to Monet of 14 July 1897, quoted in Jean-Aubry 1968, p.157.

### 4. TROUVILLE: LA REINE DES PLAGES

1. Manuscript in Villa Montebello, Musée de Trouville, Trouville. Excerpts quoted in 'Le premier Casino de Trouville', *Bulletin de la Société d'Etudes Trouvillaises*, No. 7, June 1938, pp.1–2.
2. Ibid.
3. In *L'Illustration*, 7 September 1844, quoted in exhibition catalogue, *Mozin*, p.79.

### 5. BAINS DE MER

1. 'Of all the flowers it is the human flower which has the greatest need of sunlight.' Michelet, quoted in Georges Maze, *Trouville-Deauville et environs*, Rouen, 1913, p.35.
2. 'To sunbathe is as good as a meal.' Dr Gérard, quoted in Maze, p.35.
3. Quoted in J.F.Masse, 'Esquisse pour une histoire des bains de mer', *Athena*, No. 71, March 1982, p.8.
4. Masse, pp.8–9.
5. Quoted in the Institut français d'architecture volume, *Trouville*, published by Mardaga, Brussels, 1989, p.23. Henceforth this publication will be referred to in these notes as 'Mardaga'.
6. Quoted in Christopher Marsden, *The English at the Seaside*, London, 1947, p.9.
7. Marsden, p.10.
8. Quoted in Gabriel Désert, *La vie quotidienne sur les plages normandes du Second Empire aux années folles*, Hachette, 1983.
9. Désert, p.21.
10. Quoted in Paul Morand, *Bains de mer, bains de rêve*, Paris, 1990, p.58.
11. Alphonse Karr writing in 1841, quoted in Paul Jarry, 'Bains de mer du temps passé', *Bulletin de la Société d'Etudes Trouvillaises*, No. 6, April 1938, p.9.
12. *Guide-Annuaire à Trouville-Deauville et aux environs*, Paris, 1866, pp.55–6.
13. Information from J. Chennebenoist, 'La Ligne ferroviare de Lisieux à Trouville-Deauville, jusqu'à la "Belle Epoque" ', *Athena*, No. 36, June 1973.
14. Information from Arsène Durand and Pierre Josserand, *Essai sur Trouville*, Trouville, n.d.
15. Baedeker, *Northern France from Belgium and the English Channel to the Loire*, 1889, p.152.
16. Baedeker, p.153.
17. A.R.Hope-Moncrieff (ed.), *Where to Go Abroad, A Guide to the Watering-places and Health Resorts of Europe, the Mediterranean . . .*, London, 1893, p.305.

### 6. BOUDIN AND TROUVILLE

1. Castagnary, *Salon de 1869*, quoted in Jean-Aubry, 1922, p.181.
2. Letter to Braquaval of 26 July 1894, quoted in Manoeuvre, pp.209–10.
3. Letter to F. Martin of 20 November 1884, quoted in Jean-Aubry, 1968, p.102.
4. Letter to Braquaval of 3 September 1889, quoted in Manoeuvre, p.204.
5. Letter to Braquaval of 25 October 1889, quoted in Manoeuvre, p.204.

### 7. BEACH-SCENES

1. Castagnary, *Salon de 1875*, quoted in Jean-Aubry, 1922, p.181.
2. Letter to L. Boudin of 29 November 1865, quoted in Jean-Aubry, 1968, p.60.
3. Letter to F. Martin of 12 February 1863, quoted in Jean-Aubry, 1968, p.50.
4. Letter to F. Martin of 1 June 1864, quoted in Jean-Aubry, 1968, p.50.
5. Letter to F. Martin of 6 September 1864, original letter in Bibliothèque Doucet, Paris.
6. Letter of 28 October 1881, quoted in Venturi, p.78.
7. Cahen, p.183.
8. Letter to F. Martin of 12 February 1863, quoted in Jean-Aubry, 1968, p.50.
9. Mardaga, pp.377–99.
10. Further information on Casino in article noted in Chapter 4, note 1 above, *Bulletin*, No. 7, 1938, pp.1–2.
11. Mardaga, p.377.
12. Mardaga, p.378.
13. Baedeker, 1889, p.153.
14. Mardaga, pp.381–3.
15. Baedeker, 1889, p.152.
16. Maze, p.38.
17. K.Baedeker, *Le Nord de la France jusqu'à la Loire, excepte Paris*, Paris and Leipzig, 1884, p.189.
18. Hope-Moncrieff, p.305.
19. Alfred Leroy, *The Empress Eugénie*, London, 1969, p.134.
20. Erna Barschak, *The Innocent Empress: An Intimate Study of Eugénie*, New York, 1943, p.136.
21. Mardaga, pp.353–5.
22. Cahen, p.186.
23. From Boudin's Journal, quoted in Manoeuvre, p.184.
24. Cahen, p.191.
25. From Boudin's Journal, quoted in Cahen, p.191.
26. Letter to L. Boudin, quoted in Manoeuvre, p.185.
27. Journal notes quoted in Cahen, p.194.
28. Letter to F. Martin of 28 August 1867, quoted in Jean-Aubry, 1968, p.65.
29. Letters from F. Martin to Boudin, quoted in exhibition catalogue, *Boudin*, Honfleur, 1992, p.83.
30. Letter to F. Martin of 3 September 1868, quoted in Jean-Aubry, 1968, p.72.
31. Maze, p.52.
32. Hope-Moncrieff, p.305.
33. From Boudin's Journal, quoted in de Knyff, p.42.

### 8. JETTIES

1. Castagnary, *Salon de 1868*, quoted in Jean-Aubry, 1922, p.181.
2. Boudin notebook, Cahen, p.183.
3. Letter to F. Martin of 6 July 1884, quoted in Manoeuvre, p.200.
4. Cahen, pp.182 and 185.
5. Letter to Ricada of 16 September 1888, quoted in Manoeuvre, 1992, p.203.
6. Letter from Monet to Boudin of 3 June 1859, quoted in Jean-Aubry, 1968, p.35.
7. Letter to F. Martin of 16 December 1869, quoted in Jean-Aubry, 1968, p.79.

### 9. THE PORT

1. Duranty, *Salon de 1877*, quoted in Manoeuvre, p.196.
2. Letter to F. Martin of 26 February 1875, quoted in Jean-Aubry, 1968, pp.89–90.
3. Quoted in Jean-Aubry, 1922, pp.184–5.

### 10. THE FISHMARKET

1. Auguste Dalligny, *Journal des Arts*, 13 March 1891, quoted in de Knyff, p.230.
2. Mardaga, p.321.
3. Maze, p.43.
4. Boudin notebook entries quoted in Cahen, pp.183–4.
5. Cahen, p.192.

### 12. LANDSCAPES

1. Gustave Geffroy, quoted in Jean-Aubry, 1922, p.185.
2. Letter to Braquaval of 12 September 1890, transcript in private collection.

### 13. FASHIONABLE DRESS AND BOUDIN

1. Edward Philpott, *Crinolines in our Parks and Promenades from 1710 to 1864*, London, 1864.
2. Alan Bott and Irene Clephane, *Our Mothers*, London, 1932, p.116.
3. Ibid.
4. Phillis Cunnington and Alan Mansfield, *English Costume for Sports and Outdoor Recreation*, London, 1969, p.264.

### 14. BOUDIN'S WATERCOLOURS OF BEACHES

1. Several works are preserved in the Département des Arts Graphiques des Musées du Louvre et d'Orsay.
2. Letter to F. Martin of 3 September 1868, Paris, Bibliothèque d'Art et d'Archéologie, Ms.212.
3. Ibid.
4. Letter of 9 September 1868, noted by Jean-Aubry in his manuscript notes, private collection.
5. Boudin account-books, private collection.
6. Musée Marmottan, Paris. Because of à catalogue error this work has previously been wrongly dated to 1863.
7. Letter to Braquaval of 30 June 1894, private collection.
8. De Knyff, p.368.
9. Letter to L. Boudin of 1 June 1864, private collection.
10. Cahen, p.52. Jongkind is referring to his folio of six etchings: *Vues de Hollande*.
11. Letter to F. Martin of 23 May 1869, Bibliothèque d'Art et d'Archéologie.

12. Ibid.
13. Letter to van der Velde of 5 April 1888, Le Havre, Archives Municipales.
14. Boudin's notebook for 1887, quoted in Cahen, p.197.
15. Boudin's notebook, undated, quoted in Cahen, p.185.
16. Cahen, p.183.
17. Letter to F. Martin of 25 April 1869, Bibliothèque d'Art et d'Archéologie.
18. Letter to F. Martin of 14 June 1869, ibid.
19. Letter to L. Boudin of 29 November 1865, private collection.
20. 1890, private collection.

# Bibliography

Only major printed sources consulted are given below; more extensive Boudin bibliographies can be found in the various editions of Jean-Aubry's monograph and in Robert Schmit's *catalogue raisonné*. There is a wealth of unpublished material in the Salle de documentation in the Musée d'Orsay and the Cabinet des dessins in the Louvre; in the Bibliothèque d'Art et d'Archéologie (Doucet), Paris, and in the Cabinet des estampes in the Bibliothèque Nationale, Paris. Material on the early history of bathing and on Trouville itself is preserved in the archives of the Musée de Trouville.


BOUDIN
(*in chronological order*)

Baudelaire, Charles, *Lettres à M. le Directeur de la Revue française sur le Salon de 1859*, *Revue française*, 10 and 20 June, 10 and 20 July, 1859.
Duranty, Edmond, 'Réflexions d'un bourgeois sur le Salon', *Gazette des Beaux-Arts*, Vol. XV, pp. 566–7; Vol. XVI, p. 55.
Drumont, Edouard, 'Exposition Eugène Boudin', in *La Liberté*, 4 February 1883.
Burty, Philippe, 'L'Exposition Boudin', in *La République française*, 8 February 1883.
Geffroy, Gustave, 'Eugène Boudin', in *La Justice*, 15 February 1883.
Leroi, Paul, 'Le Salon de 1887', *L'Art*, Vol. XLIII, pp. 30–43.
Buhot, Felix, *Préface du catalogue de l'exposition de 1889*.
Wyzewa, Théodor de, 'Eugène Boudin', in *L'Art dans les Deux Mondes*, 8 July 1889.
Roger-Miles, Roger, 'Eugène Boudin', *L'Eclair*, 13 August 1898.
*Atelier Eugène Boudin. Catalogue des tableaux, pastels, aquarelles et dessins, dont la vente après décès aura lieu... les 20 et 21 mars 1899*, Hôtel Drouot, Paris, Préface d'Arsène Alexandre.
Bouyer, Raymond, 'Eugène Boudin', *Gazette des Beaux-Arts*, Vol. I, pp. 117–24.
Fontainas, André, 'Art moderne. Exposition Eugène Boudin', *Mercure de France*, No. 110, February 1899, pp. 536–7.
Geffroy, Gustave, 'Eugène Boudin', *Le Journal*, 14 January 1899.
Pierrefitte, Soudan de, 'Eugène Boudin', *Le Petit Normand*, Special Number, 8 July 1900.
Cahen, Gustave, *Eugène Boudin, sa vie et son oeuvre*, preface by Arsène Alexandre, Paris, 1900.
Jean-Aubry, Gérard, 'Eugène Boudin et Claude Monet', *Havre-Eclair*, 1 August 1911.
Frantz, Henri, 'A painter of the sea: Eugène Boudin', *The Studio*, February 1912, pp. 20–8.
Jean-Aubry, Gérard, *Eugène Boudin. La vie et l'oeuvre d'après les lettres et les documents inédits*, Paris, 1922. Further editions, Neuchâtel, 1968, Paris, 1987, with the collaboration of Robert Schmit; English translation by Catherine Tisdall, 1969.
Tabarant, 'Eugène Boudin', *Bulletin de la vie artistique*, 1 July 1924, pp. 292–4.
Jean-Aubry, Gérard, 'Eugène Boudin. Notes d'un voyage en Bretagne', *Mercure de France*, 15 July 1924, pp. 325–53.
Roger-Marx, Claude, *Eugène Boudin*, Paris, 1927.
Cario, Louis, *Eugène Boudin*, Paris, 1928.
Benjamin, Ruth L., *Eugène Boudin*, New York, 1937.
Leite, José Roberto Teixeira, *Boudin no Brasil*, Rio de Janeiro, 1961.
Chennebenoist, Jean, 'Eugène Boudin', *Athena*, December 1965, n. p.
Gottlieb, Carla, 'Boudin's Drawings', *Master Drawings*, Vol. 4, Winter 1968, pp. 399–400.
Cogniat, Raymond, 'Boudin, ou le charme de l'ephémère', *Bulletin de la Société des Amis du Musée de Honfleur*, 1971, pp. 5–6.
Knyff, Gilbert de, *Eugène Boudin, raconté par lui-même, sa vie – son atelier – son oeuvre*, Paris, 1976.
Schmit, Robert, *Eugène Boudin, catalogue raisonné de l'oeuvre peint*, Paris, 1973, suppl., Paris, 1984.
Melot, Michel, *L'oeuvre gravé de Boudin, Corot, Daubigny, Dupre, Jongkind, Millet, Rousseau*, Paris, 1978.
Lemoine, P., *Boudin roi des ciels*, Lausanne, 1981.
Selz, Jean, *Eugène Boudin*, Paris, 1983; English ed. 1986.
Delouche, Denise, *Eugène Boudin et la Bretagne*, URSA, 1987.
Cohen, Françoise, *Eugène Boudin*, Musée des Beaux-Arts André Malraux, Le Havre, 1990.
Manoeuvre, Laurent, *Eugène Boudin, dessins*, Paris, 1991.
Manoeuvre, Laurent, *Boudin et la Normandie*, Paris, 1991.

BOUDIN: EXHIBITION CATALOGUES
(*in chronological order*)

*Eugène Boudin*, Marlborough Fine Art, London, 1958.
*Boudin en Bretagne*, Rennes, 1964.
*Boudin. Aquarelles et pastels*, Louvre, Paris, 1965.
*Boudin*, Paris, Galerie Schmit, 1965.
*Louis Eugène Boudin: precursor of Impressionism*, Santa Barbara Museum of Art, 1976.
*Sur les pas d'Eugène Boudin, Le Havre, Honfleur, Trouville et autres lieux*, Le Havre, Musée des Beaux-Arts, 1978.
*Boudin*, Bremen, Kunsthalle, 1979.
*Boudin*, Marcq-en-Baroeul, Fondation Anne et

Albert Prouvost, 1980.
*Boudin*, Paris, Galerie Schmit, 1980.
*Boudin*, New York, Knoedler and Co. Inc., 1981.
*Boudin and Jongkind*, Noortman & Brod, Maastricht and London, 1983–4.
*Boudin*, Paris, Galerie Schmit, 1984.
*Boudin*, Le Havre, Musée des Beaux-Arts, 1987.
*Boudin, dessins inédits*, Paris, Musée d'Orsay, 1987.
*Boudin en Cornouaille*, Quimper, Musée des Beaux-Arts, 1988.
*Boudin*, Limoges, Musée Municipal de l'Evêché, 1989.
*Boudin, Impressionist Marine Paintings*, Peabody Museum of Salem, 1991.
*Boudin*, Honfleur, Musée Eugène Boudin, 1992.

GENERAL BOOKS ON THE PERIOD

Allem, Maurice, *La Vie quotidienne sous le second Empire*, Paris, 1948.
Bailly-Herzberg, Janine, and Fidell-Beaufort, Madeleine, *Daubigny: la vie et l'oeuvre*, Paris, 1975.
Barschak, Erna, *The Innocent Empress: An Intimate Study of Eugénie*, New York, 1943.
Burnand, Robert, *La Vie quotidiennne en France de 1870 à 1900*, Paris, 1947.
Carette, Mme, *My mistress, The Empress Eugénie or Court Life at the Tuileries*, 2nd. ed. transl., London, 1889.
Champa, Kermit Swiler, *Studies in Early Impressionism*, New Haven and London, 1973.
Duveau, Georges, *La Vie ouvrière sous le second Empire*, Paris, 1946.
Exhibition catalogue, *How Impressionism Began*, Arts Council, National Museum of Wales, Cardiff, 1960.
Exhibition catalogue, *French Paintings from the Collections of Mr and Mrs Paul Mellon and Mrs Mellon Bruce*, National Gallery of Art, Washington, 1966.
Exhibition catalogue, *Jongkind*, Galerie Schmit, Paris, 1966.
Exhibition catalogue, *Jongkind and the Pre-Impressionists:Painters of the Ecole Saint-Siméon*, Sterling and Francine Clark Art Institute, Williamstown, 1977.
Exhibition catalogue, *Gustave Courbet 1819–77*, Royal Academy/Arts Council, London, 1978.
Exhibition catalogue, *L'Art en France sous le second Empire*, Grand Palais, Paris, 1979.
Exhibition catalogue, *The Realist Tradition, French Painting and Drawing 1830–1900*, Cleveland Museum of Art, Cleveland, 1980.
Exhibition catalogue, *A Day in the Country, Impressionism and the French Landscape*, Los Angeles County Museum of Art, Los Angeles, 1984.
Exhibition catalogue, *Lighting up the Landscape, French Impressionism and Its Origins*, National Gallery of Scotland, Edinburgh, 1986.
Exhibition catalogue, *The New Painting: Impressionism 1874–86*, Fine Art Museum, San Francisco, National Gallery of Art, Washington, 1986.
Exhibition catalogue, *Avant l'Impressionnisme: le préimpressionnisme à Honfleur, 1820–70*, Honfleur, 1991.
Exhibition catalogue, *French Impressionism: Treasures from the Midlands*, Birmingham Museum & Art Gallery, 1991.
Exhibition catalogue, Patrick Noon, *Richard Parkes Bonington, 'On the Pleasure of Painting'*, Yale Center for British Art, New Haven, 1991.
Exhibition catalogue, *The Rise of Landscape Painting in France, Corot to Monet*, The Currier Gallery of Art, Manchester, New Hampshire, 1991.
Hefting, Victorine, *Jongkind, D'Après sa correspondance*, Utrecht, 1969.
Filon, Augustin, *Souvenirs sur l'Impératrice Eugénie*, Paris, n. d.
Hellebranth, Robert, *Charles-François Daubigny 1817–78*, Morges, 1976.
Jollivet, Gaston, *Souvenirs de la vie de plaisir sous le second Empire*, Paris, 1927.
Kurtz, Harold, *The Empress Eugénie 1826–1920*, London, 1964.
Lemaire, Solange, 'Centenaire de Baudelaire. Baudelaire à Honfleur', *Bulletin de la Société des Amis de Musée de Honfleur*, 1968, pp. 5–12.
Lemaire, Solange, 'L'Hostellerie de Saint-Siméon, Berceau de L'Impressionnisme', *Le Pays d'Auge*, July 1986.
Leprohon, Pierre, *Les Peintres de la Côte Normande*, 1982.
Leroy, Alfred, *The Empress Eugénie*, London, 1969.
Lindon, Raymond, 'Eugène Le Poittevin et ses "Bains de Mer à Etretat" ', *Gazette des Beaux-Arts*, December 1967, pp. 349–57.
Monneret, Sophie, *L'Impressionnisme et son époque, Dictionnaire International*, 2 vols., Paris, 1978 and 1979.
Peat, Anthony North, *Paris sous le second Empire*, Paris, 1911.
Pharaon, Florian, *26,27,28,29,30 août 1867, Voyage Impérial dans le Nord de la France*, Lille [1867].
Pillement, Georges, *Les Pré-Impressionnistes*, Milan, 1974.
Poulain-Corbion, J. M., *Récit du voyage de leurs majestés l'empereur et l'impératrice en Normandie et en Bretagne*, août 1858, Paris [1858].
Rene-Lafargue, Th., *L'Impératrice Eugénie et ses femmes*, Paris, 1938.
Rewald, John, *The History of Impressionism*, 4th ed., London, 1973.
Stoeckl, Agnes de, *When Men Had Time to Love*, London, 1953.
Venturi, Lionello, *Les Archives de l'Impressionnisme*, Paris and New York, 2 vols., 1939.

TROUVILLE
*(in chronological order)*

[C. de Baudre], *Trouville et ses environs, Guide du voyageur*, 1844.
*Trouville et son avenir*, Paris, 1865.
[Henri Letang], *Guide-Annuaire à Trouville-Deauville et aux environs*, Paris, 1866. 2nd ed. with Villers-sur-Mer & Cabourg, Paris, 1868.
Vaht, B. de, *Guide Pittoresque de Trouville à Honfleur offert aux baigneurs et aux touristes*, Honfleur, 1868.
Eudel, Paul, *Trouville-Deauville, revue de la saison dite au Parc et Grand Casino. . .*, Trouville, 1881.
Enault, Louis, *Deauville*, 1882.
Baedeker, K., *Le Nord de la France jusqu'à la Loire, excepté Paris*, Leipzig and Paris, 1884. Further edition, 1887.
Baedeker, K., *Northern France from Belgium and the English Channel to the Loire*, 1889.
Joanne, P., *Normandie*, Paris, 1891.
*Guides Pratiques Conty: La Normandie*, Paris [1901–2].
Maze, Georges, *Trouville-Deauville et environs*, Rouen, 1913.

'Le premier Casino de Trouville', *Bulletin de la Société d'Etudes Trouvillaises*, No. 7, June 1938, pp. 1–2.
'Flaubert à Trouville', *Bulletin de la Société d'Etudes Trouvillaises*, No. 10, April 1939, pp. 4–10.
Extract from novel published in 1875 by Ernest Feydau, with descriptions of Trouville, *Bulletin de la Société d'Etudes Trouvillaises*, No. 11, July 1939, pp. 10–12.
Chennebenoist, Jean, *Trouville et Deauville vus par Charles Mozin, 1806–62*, Deauville, 1962.
Chennebenoist, Jean, 'La Ligne ferroviare de Lisieux à Trouville-Deauville jusqu'à la "Belle Epoque"', *Athena sur la Touques*, June 1973.
Bellonguet, Maurice, 'Les Origines de la Ligne de Chemin de Fer de Pont-L'Evêque-Trouville', *Athena*, March 1978.
Hamel, Henri, series of articles on 'Le Canton de Trouville-sur-Mer vu par des artistes', *Athena*, December 1981, pp. 15–32; September 1982, 1983, 1984.
Chennebenoist, Jean, and Davy, Michel, *Trouville: son histoire, depuis les origines connues jusqu'en 1830*, 1986.
Culot, Maurice, and Jakovljevic, Nada (eds.), *Trouville*, Institut français d'architecture, Collection Villes, Mardaga, Brussels, 1989.
Durand, Arsène, and Josserand, Pierre, *Essai sur Trouville*, Trouville, n. d.

BAINS DE MER
*(in chronological order)*
Le Coeur, M. J., *Des Bains de Mer: Guide médical et hygiènique du baigneur*, Caen, 1846, 2 vols.
Blanquet, Albert, *Les bains de mer des côtes normandes, guide pittoresque*, Paris, 1859.
Otter, R. H., *Winters Abroad*, London, 1882.
Hope-Moncrieff, A. R. (ed.), *Where to Go Abroad: A Guide to the Watering-places and Health Resorts of Europe, the Mediterranean . . .*, London, 1893.
Linn, Thomas, *The Health Resorts of Europe*, London, 1894.
Hobhouse, E., *Health Abroad*, 1899.
Weber & Weber, *Climatotherapy and Balneotherapy*, London, 1907.
*A Handbook for Travellers on the Continent: Continental Health Resorts*, 1908.
Engerand, Fernand, *Les Amusements des villes d'eaux à travers les ages*, Paris, 1936.
Jarry, Paul, 'Bains de mer du temps passé', *Bulletin de la Société d'Etudes Trouvillaises*, No. 6, April 1938, pp. 7–11.
Marsden, Christopher, *The English at the Seaside*, London, 1947.
Stokes, H. G., *The Very First History of the English Seaside*, London, 1947.
Gratrix, Dawson, *The Holiday Beaches of Northern France*, London, 1958.
Morand, Paul, *Bains de mer, bains de rêve*, Paris, 1960.
Exhibition catalogue, *Les Bains de mer*, Musée de Dieppe, 1961.
Hern, Anthony, *The Seaside Holiday: The History of the English Seaside Resort*, London, 1967.
Masse, J. F.,'Esquisse pour une histoire des bains de mer', *Athena*, March 1982.
Desert, Gabriel, *La Vie quotidienne sur les plages normandes du second Empire aux années folles*, Biarritz, 1983.
Exhibition catalogue, *Aux bains de mer:1830–1930*, Musée de Trouville, 1986.

# INDEX